"*I want you with me.*"

The breath caught in her throat and threatened to choke her.

"No comment, Kristi?" Shalef queried with a degree of mocking cynicism.

"As what?" Was that her voice? Even to her own ears it sounded impossibly husky. "Your mistress?"

"There are many advantages."

Her eyes met his and held them. "I don't want to be content with second best, waiting for a stolen night or two. I would rather not have you at all!"

HELEN BIANCHIN was born in New Zealand and traveled to Australia before marrying her Italian-born husband. After three years they moved, returned to New Zealand with their daughter, had two sons, then resettled in Australia. Encouraged by friends to recount anecdotes of her years as a tobacco sharefarmer's wife living in an Italian community, Helen began setting words on paper, and her first novel was published in 1975. An animal lover, she says her terrier and Persian cat regard her study as much theirs as hers.

Look out for *An Ideal Marriage* by Helen Bianchin, available in September.

When Gabbi married Benedict, it was celebrated as the wedding of the decade! Is theirs the perfect marriage? They are rich, successful, and share an intense passion. All that's missing is a baby—and true love?

Books by Helen Bianchin

HARLEQUIN PRESENTS
1423—THE STEFANOS MARRIAGE
1527—NO GENTLE SEDUCTION
1561—STORMFIRE
1601—RELUCTANT CAPTIVE
1704—PASSION'S MISTRESS
1741—DANGEROUS ALLIANCE
1809—FORGOTTEN HUSBAND

HELEN BIANCHIN

Desert Mistress

Harlequin Books

TORONTO • NEW YORK • LONDON
AMSTERDAM • PARIS • SYDNEY • HAMBURG
STOCKHOLM • ATHENS • TOKYO • MILAN
MADRID • WARSAW • BUDAPEST • AUCKLAND

ISBN 0-373-11872-4

DESERT MISTRESS

First North American Publication 1997.

Copyright © 1996 by Helen Bianchin.

This edition published by arrangement with Harlequin Books S.A.

Printed in U.S.A.

CHAPTER ONE

KRISTI put the finishing touches to her make-up, then stood back from the mirror to scrutinise her reflected image. An image she had deliberately orchestrated to attract one man's attention. That it would undoubtedly gain the interest of many men was immaterial.

The dress she'd chosen was fashioned in indigo raw silk; its deceptively simple cut emphasised her generously moulded breasts and narrow waist, and provided a tantalising glimpse of silk-clad thigh. Elegant high-heeled shoes completed the outfit.

Dark auburn hair fell to her shoulders in a cascade of natural curls, and cosmetic artistry highlighted wide-spaced, topaz-flecked hazel eyes, accented a delicate facial bone structure and defined a sensuously curved mouth. Jewellery was kept to a minimum—a slim-line gold watch, bracelet and earstuds.

Satisfied, Kristi caught up her evening coat, collected her purse and exited the hotel suite.

Downstairs the doorman hailed her a taxi with one imperious sweep of his hand, and once seated she gave the driver a Knightsbridge address, then sank back in contemplative silence as the vehicle eased into the flow of traffic.

The decision to travel to London had been her own, despite advice from government officials in both Australia and England that there was little to be gained in the shift of location. *'Wait,'* she'd been cautioned, 'and allow them to do their job.'

Except she'd become tired of waiting, tired of hearing different voices intoning the same words endlessly day after day. She wanted action. Action that Sheikh Shalef bin Youssef Al-Sayed might be able to generate, given that his assistance with delicate negotiations in a similar situation more than a year ago had resulted in the successful release of a hostage.

The slim hope that she might be able to persuade him to use his influence to set her brother free had been sufficient for her to book the next available flight to London and arrange accommodation.

Yet in the two weeks since her arrival Kristi's telephone calls had been politely fielded, her faxes ignored. Even baldly turning up at his suite of offices had met with failure. The man was virtually inaccessible, his privacy guarded from unwanted intrusion.

Kristi's long-standing friendship with Georgina Harrington, the daughter of a foreign diplomat, with whom she'd attended boarding-school, provided the opportunity to meet the Sheikh on a social level. There could be no doubt that without Sir Alexander Harrington's help she would never have gained an invitation to tonight's soirée.

The decision to replace Georgina with Kristi as Sir Alexander's partner had been instigated by a telephone call to the Sheikh's secretary, and had been closely followed by a fax notifying him that Georgina had fallen prey to a virulent virus and would not be able to attend. It had gone on to ask if there would be any objection to Kristi Dalton, aged twenty-seven, a friend of long-standing, taking Georgina's place. Details for security purposes were supplied. Acknowledgement together with an acceptance had been faxed through the following day.

The taxi cruised through the streets, the glisten of recent rain sparkling beneath the headlights. London in winter was vastly different from the Southern hemispheric temperatures of Australia, and for a moment she thought longingly of bright sunshine, blue skies and the sandy beaches gracing Queensland's tropical coast.

It didn't take long to reach Sir Alexander's elegant, three-storeyed apartment, and within minutes of paying off the taxi she was drawn into the lounge and handed a glass containing an innocuous mix of lime, lemonade and bitters.

'Ravishing, darling,' Georgina accorded with genuine admiration for Kristi's appearance—a compliment which was endorsed by Sir Alexander.

'Thank you,' Kristi acknowledged with a slightly abstracted smile.

So much rested on the next few hours. In her mind she had rehearsed precisely how she would act, what she would say, until the imagery almost assumed reality. There could be no room for failure.

'I've instructed Ralph to have the car out front at five-thirty,' Sir Alexander informed her. 'When you have finished your drink, my dear, we will leave.'

Kristi felt the knot of tension tighten in her stomach, and she attempted to disguise her apprehension as Georgina gave her a swift hug.

'Good luck. I'll ring you tomorrow and we'll get together for lunch.'

Sir Alexander's car was an aged Rolls, the man behind the wheel a valued servant who had been with the Harrington family for so many years that employer and employee had given up trying to remember the number.

'The traffic is light, sir,' Ralph intoned as he eased the large vehicle forward. 'I estimate we will reach the Sheikh's Berkshire manor in an hour.'

It took precisely three minutes less, Kristi noted as they slowed to a halt before a massive set of wrought-iron gates flanked by two security guards.

Ralph supplied their invitation and sufficient proof of identity, then, as the gates swung open, he eased the Rolls towards the main entrance where they were greeted by yet another guard.

'Miss Dalton. Sir Harrington. Good evening.'

To the inexperienced eye he appeared to be one of the hired help. Given the evening's occasion, there was a valid reason for the mobile phone held in one hand. Yet the compilation of information that Kristi had accumulated about his employer left her in little doubt that there was a regulation shoulder-holster beneath his suit jacket, his expertise in the field of martial arts and marksmanship a foregone conclusion.

A butler stood inside the heavily panelled front door, and Kristi relinquished her coat to him before being led at Sir Alexander's side by a delegated hostess to join fellow guests in a room that could only have been described as sumptuous.

Gilt-framed mirrors and original works of art graced silk-covered walls, and it would have been sacrilege to suggest that the furniture was other than French antique. Multi-faceted prisms of light were reflected from three exquisite crystal chandeliers.

'I'll have one of the waiters bring you something to drink. If you'll excuse me?'

An elaborate buffet was presented for personal selection, and there were several uniformed waitresses circling the room, carrying trays laden with gourmet hors d'oeuvres.

Muted background music was barely distinguishable beneath the sound of chattering voices, and Kristi's smile was polite as Sir Alexander performed an introduction to the wife of an English earl who had recently presented her husband with a long-awaited son.

Kristi scanned the room idly, observing fellow guests with fleeting interest. Black dinner suit, crisp white cotton shirt and black bow-tie were *de rigueur* for the men, and her experienced eye detected a number of women wearing designer gowns whose hair and make-up bore evidence of professional artistry.

Her gaze slid to a halt, arrested by a man whose imposing height and stature set him apart from everyone else in the room.

Sheikh Shalef bin Youssef Al-Sayed.

Newspaper photographs and coloured prints in the pages of glossy magazines didn't do him justice, for in the flesh he exuded an animal sense of power—a physical magnetism that was riveting.

An assemblage of finely honed muscle accented a broad bone structure, and his facial features bore the sculpted prominence of inherited genes. Dark, well-groomed hair and olive skin proclaimed the stamp of his paternal lineage.

Information regarding his background gleaned from press releases depicted him as the son of an Arabian prince and an English mother—a woman who, it was said, had agreed to an Islamic wedding ceremony which had never been formalised outside Saudi Arabia, and after a brief sojourn in her husband's palace had fled back to England where she'd steadfastly refused, despite giving birth to a much coveted son, to return to a country where women were subservient to men and took second place to an existing wife.

Yet the love affair between the Prince and his English wife had continued to flourish during his many visits to London, until her untimely death, whereupon the ten-year-old Shalef had been removed from England by his father and introduced to his Arabian heritage.

Now in his late thirties, Shalef bin Youssef Al-Sayed had won himself international respect among his peers for his entrepreneurial skills, and in the years since his father's demise his name had become synonymous with immense wealth.

A man no sensible person would want as an enemy, Kristi perceived wryly. Attired in a a superbly cut evening suit, there was an elemental ruthlessness beneath his sophisticated façade.

As if some acute sense alerted him to her scrutiny, he lifted his head, and for a few timeless seconds his eyes locked with hers.

The room and its occupants seemed to fade to the periphery of her vision as she suffered his raking appraisal, and she was unable to control the slow heat coursing through her veins. Intense awareness vibrated from every nerve cell, lifting the fine body hairs on the surface of her skin.

No man of her acquaintance had made her feel so acutely vulnerable, and she found the sensation disconcerting. Had it been any other man, she would have displayed no interest and openly challenged his veiled evaluation. With Shalef bin Youssef Al-Sayed she couldn't allow herself the luxury of doing so.

For one split second she glimpsed lurking cynicism in his expression, then his attention was diverted by a man who greeted him with the earnest deference of the emotionally insecure.

The study of body language had been an integral part of her training as a photographer, inasmuch as she'd consciously chosen to emphasise the positive rather than the negative in the posed, still shots that had provided her bread and butter in the early days of her career in her parents' Double Bay photographic studio.

Kristi's gaze lingered, her interest entirely professional. Or so she told herself as she observed the slant of Shalef bin Youssef Al-Sayed's head, the movement of his sensually moulded mouth as he engaged in polite conversation, the piercing directness of his gaze. To the unwary he appeared totally relaxed, yet there was tensile steel apparent in his stance, a silent strength that was entirely primitive. And infinitely dangerous.

A feather of fear pricked the base of her neck and slithered slowly down the length of her spine. As an enemy he would be lethal.

'Kristi.'

She turned at the sound of her name and gave Sir Alexander a warm smile.

'Allow me to introduce Annabel and Lance Shrewsbury.' His voice was so incredibly polite that Kristi's eyes held momentary mischief before it was quickly masked. 'Kristi Dalton, a valued friend from Australia.'

'*Australia*!' Annabel exclaimed in a voice that diminished the country to a position of geographical obscurity. 'I'm fascinated. Do you live on a farm out there?'

'Sydney,' Kristi enlightened her politely. 'A city with a population in excess of five million.' She shouldn't have resorted to wry humour, she knew, but she couldn't help adding, 'The large farms are called stations, each comprising millions of acres.'

The woman's eyes widened slightly. 'Good heavens. *Millions*?'

'Indeed,' Kristi responded solemnly. 'A plane or helicopter is used to check boundary fences and monitor stock.'

Annabel suppressed a faint shudder. 'All that red dirt, the heat, and the snakes. My dear, I couldn't live there.' Red-tipped fingers fluttered in an aimless gesture, matching in colour the red-glossed mouth, and in perfection the expensive orthodontic work, and the considerable skill of cosmetic surgery.

Thirty, going on forty-five, married to a wealthy member of the aristocracy, and born to shop, Kristi summarised, endeavouring not to be uncharitable.

'Sir Alexander.'

Awareness arrowed through her body at the sound of that smooth, well-educated drawl, and she turned slowly to greet their host.

His shirt was of the finest cotton, his dinner suit immaculately tailored to fit his broad frame, and this close she could sense the clean smell of soap mingling with the exclusive tones of his cologne.

Unbidden, her eyes were drawn to his mouth, and she briefly examined its curve and texture, stifling the involuntary query as to what it would be like to have that mouth possess her own. Heaven and hell, a silent voice taunted, dependent on his mood. There was a hint of cruelty apparent, a ruthlessness that both threatened and enticed. A man who held an undeniable attraction for women, she perceived, yet willing to be tamed by very few.

It was almost as if he was able to read her thoughts, for she glimpsed musing mockery in those slate-grey eyes—a colour that was in direct defiance of nature's genetics, and the only visible feature that gave evidence of his maternal ancestry.

'Miss Dalton.'

'Sheikh bin Al-Sayed,' Kristi acknowledged formally, aware that his gaze rested fractionally long on her hair before lowering to conduct a leisurely appraisal of her features.

It was crazy to feel intensely conscious of every single breath, every beat of her pulse. Silent anger lent her eyes a fiery sparkle, and it took considerable effort to mask it. An effort made all the more difficult as she glimpsed his amusement before he turned his attention to Sir Alexander.

'Georgina is unwell, I understand?'

'She asks me to convey her apologies,' Sir Alexander offered. 'She is most disappointed not to be able to attend this evening.'

Shalef bin Youssef Al-Sayed inclined his head. 'It is to be hoped she recovers soon.' He moved forward to speak to a woman who showed no reticence in greeting him with obvious affection.

'Would you care for another drink?'

Kristi felt as if she'd been running a marathon, and she forced herself to breathe evenly as everything in the room slid into focus. The unobtrusive presence of the waiter was a welcome distraction, and she placed her empty glass on the tray. 'Mineral water, no ice.' She didn't need the complication of a mind dulled by the effects of alcohol.

'Would you like me to get you something to eat, my dear?' Sir Alexander queried. 'Several of the guests seem to be converging on the buffet.'

Kristi summoned a warm smile as she linked her hand through his arm. 'Shall we join them? I'm feeling quite hungry.' It was a downright lie, but Sir Alexander wasn't to know that.

There was so much to choose from, she decided minutes later: hot and cold dishes, salads, hot vegetables, delicate slices of smoked salmon, seafood, chicken, turkey, roast lamb, slender cuts of beef. The selection of desserts would have put any of the finest London restaurants to shame, and the delicate ice sculptures were a visual confirmation of the chef's artistic skill.

Kristi took two slices of smoked salmon, added a small serving of three different salads, a scoop of caviare, then drifted to one side of the room.

How many guests were present tonight? she pondered idly. Fifty, possibly more? It was impossible to attempt a counting of heads, so she didn't even try.

Sir Alexander appeared to have been trapped by a society matron who seemed intent on discussing something of great importance, given the intensity of her expression.

'All alone, *chérie*? Such a crime.'

The accent was unmistakably French, and she moved slightly to allow her view to encompass the tall frame of a man whose smiling features bore a tinge of practised mockery.

'You will permit me to share a few minutes with you as we eat?'

She effected a faint shrug. 'Why not? We're fellow guests.'

'You are someone I would like to get to know—
very well.' The pause was calculated, the delicate
emphasis unmistakable.

Kristi's French was flawless, thanks to a degree
in Italian and French, her knowledge and accent
honed by a year spent in each country. 'I am
selective when it comes to choosing a friend—or a
lover, *monsieur*.' Her smile was singularly sweet.
'It is, perhaps, unfortunate that I do not intend to
remain in London long enough to devote time to
acquiring one or the other.'

'I travel extensively. We could easily meet.'

His persistence amused her. 'I think not.'

'You do not know who I am?'

'That is impossible, as we have yet to be introduced,' she managed lightly. Perhaps she presented
a challenge.

'*Enchanté, chérie.*' His eyes gleamed darkly as
he reached for her hand and raised it to his lips.
'Jean-Claude Longchamp d'Elseve.' He paused,
head tilted slightly as he waited for an expected reaction. When she failed to comply, his mouth assumed a quizzical slant. 'I cannot believe you lack
the knowledge or the intelligence to be aware of the
importance my family hold in France.'

'Really?'

He was an amusing diversion, and he was sufficiently astute to appreciate it. 'I am quite serious.'

'So am I, Jean-Claude,' she declared solemnly.

'You make no attempt to acquaint me with your
name. Does this mean I am to be rejected?' The
musing gleam in his eyes belied the wounded tone.

'Do you not handle rejection well?'

His mouth parted in subdued laughter. 'I am so rarely in such a position, it is something of a novelty.'

'I'm relieved. I would hate to provide you with an emotional scar.'

He still held her hand, and his thumb traced a light pattern over the veins of her wrist. 'Perhaps we could begin again. Will you have dinner with me?'

'The answer is still the same.'

'It will be relatively easy for me to discover where you are staying.'

'Please don't,' Kristi advised seriously.

'Why not?' His shrug was eloquent. 'Am I such objectionable company?'

She pulled her hand free. 'Not at all.' She cast him a slight smile. 'I simply have a tight business schedule and a full social calendar.'

The edge of his mouth curved in pensive humour. 'You mean to leave me to another woman's mercy?'

In different circumstances he might have proved to be an amusing companion. 'I'm sure you can cope.'

His eyes gleamed with hidden warmth. 'Perhaps. Although I may choose not to.'

'Your prerogative,' she accorded lightly. 'If you'll excuse me? I should rejoin Sir Alexander.'

Jean-Claude inclined his head and offered a teasing smile. *'Au revoir, chérie.'*

Her food had remained almost untouched, and she handed the plate to a passing waitress, her appetite gone.

Sir Alexander wasn't difficult to find, although he appeared deep in conversation with a distinguished-looking guest and she was loath to interrupt them.

'Champagne?'

Kristi cast the waitress and the tray she carried a fleeting glance. Perhaps she *should* have a glass to diffuse her nervous tension. Even as the thought occurred, she dismissed it. Coffee, strong black and sweet was what she needed, and she voiced the request, then made her way to the end of the buffet table where a uniformed maid was offering a variety of hot beverages.

Declining milk, she moved to one side and sipped the potent brew. The blend was probably excellent, but she hardly noticed as she steeled herself to instigate a planned action.

Seconds later her cup lay on the carpet, and the scalding liquid seared her midriff. The pain was intense—far more so than she'd anticipated.

'Oh, my dear, how unfortunate. Are you all right?' The voiced concern brought attention, and within minutes she was being led from the room by the hostess who had greeted them on arrival.

'We keep the first-aid equipment in a bathroom next to the kitchen.' The hostess's voice was calm as she drew Kristi down a wide hallway and into a room that was clinically functional. 'If you'll remove your dress I'll apply a cold compress to cool the skin.'

Kristi complied, adding a sodden half-slip to the heap of ruined silk, then stood silently as the hostess efficiently dealt with the burn, applied salve, then covered the area with a sterile dressing.

'I'll organise a robe and have someone take care of your dress.'

Minutes later Kristi willed the hostess a speedy return, for despite central heating the room was cool, and a lacy bra and matching wispy bikini briefs were hardly adequate covering.

A frown creased her forehead, and she unconsciously gnawed at her lower lip, uneasy now that she had implemented her plan. There was a very slim chance that Sheikh bin Al-Sayed would check on her himself. Yet she was a guest in his home, and courtesy alone should ensure that he enquired as to her welfare—surely?

Her scalded flesh stung abominably, despite the hostess's ministrations. A wide, raised welt of red skin encompassed much of her midriff and tapered off in the region of her stomach. Even she had been surprised that one cup of hot liquid was capable of covering such an area.

A sound alerted Kristi's attention an instant before the door swung inwards. Her eyes widened measurably as Shalef bin Youssef Al-Sayed stood momentarily in its aperture.

He held a white towelling robe, his features schooled into a fathomless mask, and she shivered, unable to control the slither of apprehension as he moved into the room and closed the door.

Its soft clunking sound was somehow significant, and her hands moved instinctively to cover her breasts.

'I suggest you put this on. It would be unfortunate to compound your accident with a chill.'

The room suddenly seemed much smaller, his height and breadth narrowing its confines to a degree where she felt stifled and painfully aware of the scarcity of her attire.

Reaching forward, she took the robe and quickly pushed her arms into the sleeves, then firmly belted the ties, only to wince and ease the knot. 'Thank you.'

'Rochelle assures me the burn, while undoubtedly painful, is not serious enough to warrant professional medical attention. Your gown is silk and may not fare well when cleaned. Replace it and send me the bill.'

'That won't be necessary,' Kristi said stiffly.

'I insist.' His gaze was startlingly direct, and difficult for her to hold.

'It was a simple accident, and the responsibility is entirely mine,' she declared, hating her body's reaction to his presence. It had been bad enough in a room full of people. Alone with him, it was much worse.

His eyes narrowed. 'You decline the replacement of an expensive dress?'

'I don't seek an argument with you.'

With easy economy of movement he slid one hand into a trouser pocket—an action which parted the superbly tailored dinner jacket and displayed an expanse of snowy white cotton shirt, beneath which it was all too easy to imagine a taut midriff and steel-muscled chest liberally sprinkled with dark, springy hair.

'What precisely is it that you do seek, Miss Dalton?' The words were a quizzical drawl laced with cynicism.

There was an implication, thinly veiled, that succeeded in tightening the muscles supporting her spine. It also lifted her chin and brought a brightness to her eyes.

His smile was totally lacking in humour. 'All evening I have been intrigued by the method you would choose to attract my attention.' His mouth assumed a mocking slant. 'No scenario I envisaged included a self-infliction of injury.'

CHAPTER TWO

KRISTI felt the color drain from her face. 'How dare you suggest—?'

'Save your breath, Miss Dalton. An investigation fell into place immediately after your second phone call to my office,' Shalef bin Youssef Al-Sayed informed her with deadly softness. His gaze never left her features as he listed the schools she'd attended, her educational achievements, her parents' names and the cause of their accidental death, her address, occupation, and a concise compilation of her inherited assets. 'Your visit to London was precipitated by a desire to accelerate the release of your brother, Shane, who is currently being held hostage in a remote mountain area,' he concluded in the same silky tones.

Anger surged through her veins, firing a helpless fury. 'You *knew* why I was trying to contact you, yet you denied me the courtesy of accepting one of my calls?'

'There seemed little point. I cannot help you, Miss Dalton.'

The words held a finality that Kristi refused to accept. 'Shane was unfortunate to be in the wrong place at the wrong time—'

'Your brother is a professional news photographer who ignored advice and flouted legal sanction

22

in order to enter a forbidden area,' Shalef bin Youssef Al-Sayed declared hardly. 'He was kidnapped by an opposing faction and taken beyond reach of local authorities, who would surely have instigated his arrest and incarcerated him in prison.'

'You consider his fate is better with a band of political dissidents?'

His mouth curved into a mere facsimile of a smile. 'That is debatable, Miss Dalton.'

Concern widened her eyes and robbed her features of their colour. The image of her brother being held captive kept her awake nights; then, when she did manage to sleep, her mind was invaded by nightmares. 'I implore you—'

'You beg very prettily,' Shalef bin Youssef Al-Sayed taunted mercilessly, and in that moment she truly hated him. 'However, I suggest you direct all your enquiries through the appropriate channels. Such negotiations take time and require the utmost delicacy. And patience,' he added with slight emphasis. 'On the part of the hostage's family.'

'You could help get him out,' she declared in impassioned entreaty.

His gaze speared through her body and lanced her very soul, freezing her into speechlessness. There was scarcely a sound in the room, only the whisper of her breathing and she couldn't have looked away from him if she'd tried.

'We are close to the twenty-first century, Miss Dalton,' he drawled. 'You did not imagine I would don a *thobe* and *gutra*, mount an Arab steed and ride into the desert on a rescue mission with men following on horseback, taking water and food from conveniently placed oases along the way?'

Kristi ignored his sardonic cynicism, although it cost her considerable effort not to launch a verbal attack. 'I have a sizeable trust fund which is easily accessed,' she assured him with determined resolve, grateful in this instance for inherited wealth. 'Sufficient to cover the cost of hiring Jeeps, men, a helicopter if necessary.'

'No.'

The single negation sparked a feeling of desperation. She held one ace up her sleeve, but this wasn't the moment to play it. 'You refuse to help me?'

'Go home, Miss Dalton.' His expression was harsh, and his voice sounded as cold as if it had come direct from the North Pole. 'Go back to Australia and let the governments sort out the unfortunate incident.'

She wanted to hit him, to lash out physically and berate him for acting like an unfeeling monster.

He knew, and for one fraction of a second his eyes flared, almost as if in anticipation of her action—and the certain knowledge of how he would deal with it. Then the moment was gone, and it had been so swift, so fleeting that she wondered if it hadn't been a figment of her imagination.

'You will have to excuse me. I have a party to host,' he imparted with smooth detachment. 'Rochelle will bring you something suitable to wear. Should you wish to return to your hotel, it will be arranged for a driver to transport you there.

Otherwise, I can only suggest that you attempt to enjoy the rest of the evening.'

'Please.' Her voice broke with emotional intensity.

His eyes flayed every layer of protective clothing, burning skin, tissue, seeming to spear through to her very soul. With deliberate slowness he appraised her slender figure, resting over-long on the curve of her breasts, the apex between her thighs, before sweeping up to settle on the soft fullness of her mouth. 'There is nothing you can offer me as a suitable enticement.'

Anger brightened her eyes, and pride kept her head high. 'You insult my intelligence, Shalef bin Youssef Al-Sayed. I was appealing for your compassion. Sex was never a consideration.'

'You are a woman, Miss Dalton. Sex is always a consideration.'

A soft tinge of pink coloured her cheeks as she strove to keep a rein on her temper. She drew a deep, ragged breath, then released it slowly. 'Not even for my brother would I use my body as a bartering tool.'

His eyes narrowed with cynical amusement. 'No?'

She was sorely tempted to yell at him, but that would only have fuelled his amusement. 'No.' The word was quietly voiced and carried far more impact than if she'd resorted to angry vehemence.

He turned towards the door, and the blood seemed to roar in her ears, then she felt it slowly drain, leaving her disoriented and dangerously light-headed for an instant before she managed to gather some measure of control.

'What would it take for you to make a personal appeal to Mehmet Hassan on my behalf?' The words were singularly distinct, each spoken quietly, but they caused Shalef bin Youssef Al-Sayed to pause, then turn slowly to face her.

His features were assembled into an inscrutable mask, and his eyes held a wariness that was chilling.

'Who precisely is Mehmet Hassan?' The voice was dangerously quiet, the silky tones deceptive, for she sensed a finely honed anger beneath their surface.

She felt trapped by the intentness of those incredible eyes, much like a rabbit caught in the headlights of a car, and she took a deep, shuddering breath, then released it slowly. 'You attended the same school and established a friendship which exists to this day, despite Mehmet Hassan's little-known link with political dissident leaders.'

Dark lashes lowered, successfully hooding his gaze. 'I know a great many people, Miss Dalton,' he drawled, 'some of whom I number as friends.'

She had his attention. She dared not lose it.

'You travel to Riyadh several times a year on business, occasionally extending your stay to venture into the desert with a hunting party to escape from the rigours of the international corporate world. You never go alone, and it has been whispered that Mehmet Hassan has been your guest on a number of occasions.'

He was silent for what seemed to be several minutes but could only have been seconds. 'Whispers, like grains of sand, are swept far by the desert winds and retain no substance.'

'You deny your friendship with Mehmet Hassan?'

His expression hardened, his eyes resembling obsidian. 'What is the purpose of this question?'

Steady, an inner voice cautioned. 'I want you to take me with you to Riyadh.'

'Entry into Saudi Arabia requires a sponsor.'

'Something you could arrange without any effort.'

'If I was so inclined.'

'I suggest you *are* inclined,' Kristi said carefully. Shalef bin Youssef Al-Sayed's appraisal was all-encompassing as it slowly raked her slim frame. 'You would dare to threaten me?' he queried with dangerous softness, and she shivered inwardly at the ominous, almost lethal quality apparent in his stance.

'I imagine the media would be intensely interested to learn of the link between Sheikh Shalef bin Youssef Al-Sayed and Mehmet Hassan,' she opined quietly. 'Questions would undoubtedly be raised, public opinion swayed, and at the very least it would cause you embarrassment.'

'There is a very high price to pay for attempted blackmail, Miss Dalton.'

She pulled the figurative ace and played it. 'I am applying the rudiments of successful business practice. A favour in exchange for information withheld. My terms, Sheikh bin Al-Sayed, are un-restricted entry into Riyadh under your sponsor-ship. For my own protection, it is necessary for me to be a guest in your home. By whichever means you choose you will make contact with Mehmet Hassan and request his help in negotiating for my brother's release. In return, I will meet whatever expenses are incurred.' Her eyes never wavered from his. 'And pledge my silence.'

'I could disavow any knowledge of this man you call Mehmet Hassan.'

'I would know you lie.'

If he could have killed her, he would have done so. It was there in his eyes, the flexing of a taut muscle at the edge of his cheek. 'What you ask is impossible.'

A faint smile lifted the corner of her mouth. 'Difficult, but not impossible.'

The sound of a discreet knock at the door, and seconds later Rochelle entered the room with a swathe of black draped over her arm.

'Perhaps we can arrange to further this dis-cussion at a more opportune time?' Kristi offered with contrived politeness. 'It would be impolite to neglect your guests for much longer.'

Shalef bin Youssef Al-Sayed inclined his head. 'Indeed. Shall we say dinner tomorrow evening? I will send a car to your hotel at six.'

A tiny thrill of exhilaration spiralled through her body. 'Thank you.'

His eyes were hooded and his smile was barely evident. 'I shall leave you with Rochelle,' he declared formally, then, with a dismissing gesture, he moved into the passageway and closed the door behind him.

'I think these should be adequate,' Rochelle indicated as she held out the evening trousers and an elegant beaded top.

They were superb, the style emphasising Kristi's slender frame and highlighting the delicate fragility of her features.

'Do you feel ready to rejoin the party? Sir Alexander Harrington has expressed anxiety as to your welfare.'

'Thank you.'

It really was a splendid gathering, Kristi acknowledged silently some time later as she sipped an innocuous fruit punch. She had attended many social events in the past ten years in numerous capital cities around the world, with guests almost as impressive as these, in prestigious homes that were equally opulent as this one. Yet none had proved to be quite as nerve-racking.

Shalef bin Youssef Al-Sayed was not a man to suffer fools gladly. And deep inside she couldn't discount the fact that she was indeed being foolish in attempting to best him. Twice in the past hour she had allowed her gaze to scan the room casually, unconsciously seeking the autocratic features of her host among the many guests.

Even when relaxed he had an inherent ruthlessness that she found vaguely disturbing. Yet familial loyalty overrode the need for rational thought, and she dampened down a feeling of apprehension at the prospect of sharing dinner with him the following evening.

A strange prickling sensation began at the back of her neck, and some inner force made her seek its source, her gaze seeming to home in on the man who silently commanded her attention.

Dark eyes seared her own, and the breath caught in her throat for a few long seconds as she suffered his silent annihilation, then she raised one eyebrow and slanted him a polite smile before deliberately turning towards Sir Alexander.

'Would you like to leave, my dear?'

Kristi offered him a bemused look, and glimpsed his concern. 'It *is* getting late,' she agreed, moving to his side as they began circling the room to where their host stood listening to an earnest-looking couple conducting what appeared to be an in-depth conversation.

'Sir Alexander, Miss Dalton.' The voice was pleasant, the tone polite.

'It has been a most enjoyable evening,' Sir Alexander said cordially, while Kristi opted to remain silent.

'It is to be hoped the effects of your accident will be minimal, Miss Dalton,' Shalef drawled, and she responded with marked civility,

'Thank you, Sheikh bin Al-Sayed, for the borrowed clothes. I shall have them cleaned and returned to you.'

He merely inclined his head in acknowledgement, and Kristi found herself mentally counting each step that led from the lounge.

As they reached the foyer, instruction was given for the Rolls to be brought around. Within minutes they were both seated in the rear and Ralph began easing the vehicle down the long, curving driveway.

'I trust you were successful, my dear?'

Kristi turned towards Sir Alexander with a faint smile. 'To a degree, although he was aware of the deliberate orchestration. We're to dine together to-morrow evening.'

'Be careful,' he bade her seriously. 'Shalef bin Youssef Al-Sayed is not someone with whom I would choose to cross words.'

A chill finger feathered its way down her spine. A warning? 'Shane's welfare is too important for me to back down now.'

A hand covered hers briefly in conciliation. 'I understand. However, as a precaution, I would suggest you keep me abreast of any developments. I feel a certain degree of responsibility.'

'Of course.'

It was after midnight when Ralph slid the Rolls to a halt outside the main entrance to her hotel, and an hour later she lay gazing sightlessly at the darkened ceiling, unable to sleep. There was still a slight rush of adrenalin firing her brain, a feeling of victory mixed with anxiety that prevented the ability to relax. Would Shalef bin Youssef Al-Sayed present a very clever argument in opposition to her bid to have him take her to Riyadh? Call her bluff regarding her threat to inform the media of his friendship with Mehmet Hassan? She had seven-teen hours to wait before she found out.

*   *   *

Kristi stepped out of the lift at precisely five minutes to six and made her way to the foyer. It was raining heavily outside, the sky almost black, and the wind howled along the space between tall buildings and up narrow alleyways with a ferocity of sound that found its way inside each time the main entrance doors swung open.

An omen? It wasn't a night one would have chosen to venture out in, not if a modicum of common sense was involved. The occasional blast of cold air penetrated the warmth of the central heating like icy fingers reaching in to pluck out the unwary.

Kristi drew the edges of her coat together, adjusted the long woollen scarf, then plunged her hands into her capacious pockets.

Where would they dine? There was an excellent restaurant in the hotel. She would feel infinitely safer if they remained in familiar surroundings.

She watched as a black Bentley swept in beneath the portico. The driver emerged, spoke briefly to the attendant, then strode indoors to receive the concierge's attention, who, after listening intently, gave an indicative nod in Kristi's direction.

Intrigued, she waited for him to reach her.

'Miss Dalton?' He produced ID and waited patiently while she scrutinised it. 'Sheikh bin Al-Sayed has instructed me to drive you to his home in Berkshire.'

Her stomach performed a backward flip, then settled with an uneasy fluttering of nerves. *His* territory, when she'd hoped for the relative safety of a restaurant in which to conduct negotiations.

The success of her ploy rested on one single fact: information that was known to only a privileged few. Her source had extracted a vow of secrecy— a promise she intended to honour despite any threat Shalef bin Youssef Al-Sayed could throw at her.

The large vehicle escaped the city's outskirts, gathered speed, its passage becoming much too swift for Kristi's peace of mind.

It was stupid to feel so nervous, she rationalised as the Bentley slid between the heavy wrought-iron gates and progressed up the curved drive. Insane to feel afraid when the house was staffed with a complement of servants. Yet she was consumed with a measure of both when the door opened and Rochelle ushered her inside.

'May I take your coat?' With it folded across one arm, she indicated a door to her right. 'Come through to the lounge.'

The room was measurably smaller than the large, formal lounge used for last night's party, Kristi observed as she followed Rochelle's gesture and sank down into one of the several deep-seated sofas.

'Can I get you something to drink? Wine? Orange juice? Tea or coffee?'

Hot, fragrant tea sounded wonderful, and she said as much, accepting the steaming cup minutes later.

'If you'll excuse me?' Rochelle queried. 'Sheikh bin Al-Sayed will join you shortly.'

Was it a deliberate tactic on his part to keep her waiting? In all probability, Kristi conceded as she sipped the excellent brew.

He had a reputation as a powerful strategist, a man who hired and fired without hesitation in his quest for dedication and commitment from his employees. The pursuit of excellence in all things, at any cost. Wasn't that the consensus of everything she'd managed to learn about him? Admires enterprise, respects equals and dismisses fools.

But what of the man behind the image? Had the contrast between two vastly different cultures caused a conflict of interest and generated a resentment that he didn't totally belong to either? Little was known of his personal life as a child, whether his mother favoured a strict British upbringing or willingly allowed him knowledge of his father's religion and customs.

If there had been any problems, it would appear that he'd dealt with and conquered them, Kristi reflected as she replaced the cup down on its saucer.

'Miss Dalton.'

She gave a start of surprise at the sound of his voice. His entry into the room had been as silent as that of a cat.

'Sheikh bin Al-Sayed,' she acknowledged with a calmness that she was far from feeling. If she'd still been holding the cup it would have rattled as it touched the saucer.

'My apologies for keeping you waiting.'

He didn't offer a reason, and she didn't feel impelled to ask for one. Her eyes were cool and distant

as they met his, her features assembled into a mask
of deliberate politeness.

'You've finished your tea. Would you care for
some more?'

The tailored black trousers and white chambray
shirt highlighted his powerful frame—attire that
verged on the informal, and a direct contrast to the
evening suit of last night.

It made her feel overdressed, her suit too blatant
a statement with its dramatic red figure-hugging
skirt and fitted jacket. Sheer black hose and black
stilettos merely added emphasis.

'No. Thank you,' she added as she sank back
against the cushions in a determined bid to match
his detachment.

'I trust the burn no longer causes you
discomfort?'

The skin was still inflamed and slightly tender,
but there was no sign of blistering. 'It's fine.'

He accepted her assurance without comment.
'Dinner will be served in half an hour.'

'You do intend to feed me.' The words emerged
with a tinge of mockery, and she saw one of his
eyebrows slant in a gesture of cynicism.

'I clearly specified dinner.'

Kristi forced herself to conduct a silent study of
his features, observing the broad, powerfully defined cheekbones and the sensual shaping of his
mouth. Dark slate-grey eyes possessed an almost
predatory alertness, and she couldn't help wondering if they could display any real tenderness.

A woman would have to be very special to penetrate his self-imposed armour. Did he ever let down his guard, or derive enjoyment from the simple pleasures in life? In the boardroom he was regarded as an icon. And in the bedroom? There could be little doubt that he would possess the technique to drive a woman wild, but did he ever care enough to become emotionally involved? Was he, in turn, driven mad with passion? Or did he choose to distance himself?

It was something she would never know, Kristi decided with innate honesty. Something she never *wanted* to know.

'Shall we define what arrangements need to be made?' It was a bold beginning, especially when she felt anything but bold.

One eyebrow rose in a dark curve. 'We have the evening, Miss Dalton. An initial exchange of pleasantries would not be untoward, surely?' It was a statement, politely voiced, but there was steel beneath the silk. A fact she chose to heed—in part.

'Do you usually advocate wasting time during a business meeting?' Kristi proffered civilly.

'I conduct business in my office.'

'And entertain in your home?'

'Our discussion contains a politically delicate element which would be best not overheard by fellow diners, don't you agree?' he drawled, noting the tight clasp of her fingers as she laced her hands together.

She drew a deep breath and deliberately tempered its release. 'We are alone now.'

His smile held no pretension to humour. 'I suggest you contain your impatience until after dinner.'

It took a tremendous effort to contain her anger. 'If you insist.'

He registered the set of her shoulders as she unconsciously squared them, the almost prim placing of one silk-encased ankle over the other. 'Why not enjoy a light wine? Diluted, if you choose, with soda water.'

It might help her relax. She needed to, desperately. 'Thank you. Three-quarters soda.'

Why couldn't he be older, and less masculine? Less forceful, with little evidence of a raw virility that played havoc with her nervous system? Last night he had dominated a room filled with guests and succeeded in diminishing her defences. A fact she'd put down to circumstance and acute anxiety. Yet tonight she was aware that nothing had changed.

His very presence was unnerving, and she consciously fought against his physical magnetism as she accepted the glass from his hand.

'You are a photographer,' Shalef bin Youssef Al-Sayed stated as he took a comfortable chair opposite. His movements were fluid, lithe, akin to those of a large cat. 'Did you chose to follow in your brother's footsteps?'

Conversation. That's all it is, she reminded herself as she took an appreciative sip of the spritzer. It was cool and crisp to the palate, pleasant.

'Not deliberately. Shane was the older brother I adored as a child,' Kristi explained, prey to a host of images, all of them fond. 'Consequently I was intensely interested in everything he did. Photography became his obsession. Soon it was mine,' she concluded simply.

'Initially within Australia, then to various capitals throughout the world.'

'Facts you were able to access from my dossier.'

He lifted his tumbler and took a long draught of his own drink. 'A concise journalistic account.' His eyes speared hers, dark and relentless beneath the slightly hooded lids. 'Words which can't begin to convey several of the offbeat assignments you were contracted to undertake.'

'Photographs, even video coverage, don't adequately express the horror of poverty, illness and famine in some Third World countries. The hopelessness that transcends anger, the acceptance of hunger. The utter helplessness one feels at being able to do so little. The impossibility of distancing yourself from the harsh reality of it all, aware that you're only there for as long as it takes to do your job, before driving a Jeep out to the nearest airstrip and boarding a cargo shuttle that transports you back to civilisation, where you pick up your life again and attempt to pretend that what you saw, what you experienced, was just a bad dream.'

'Until the next time.'

'Until the next time,' Kristi echoed.

He surveyed her thoughtfully for several long seconds. 'You're very good at what you do.'

She inclined her head and ventured, with a touch of mockery, 'But you can't understand why I failed to settle for freelancing and filling the society pages, in a photographic studio, as my parents did.'

'The lack of challenge?'

Oh, yes. But it had been more than that—a great deal more. The photographic studio still operated, as a mark of respect for their parents, run by a competent photographer called Annie who doubled as secretary. It was an arrangement which worked very well, for it allowed Kristi freedom to pursue international assignments.

'And a desire to become your brother's equal.'

She digested his words, momentarily intrigued by a possibility that had never occurred to her until this man had voiced it. 'You make it sound as if I wanted to compete against him,' she said slowly, 'when that was never the case.'

'Yet you have chosen dangerous locations,' he pursued, watching the play of emotions on her expressive features.

Her eyes assumed a depth and dimension that mirrored her inner feelings. 'I don't board a plane and flit off to the other side of the world every second week. Sometimes there are months in between assignments, and I spend that time working out of the studio, attending social events, taking the society shots, sharing the family-portrait circuit with Annie.' She paused momentarily. 'When I undertake an assignment I want my work to matter, to encapsulate on film precisely what is needed to bring the desired result.' The passion was clearly evident in her voice, and there was a soft tinge of pink colouring her cheeks. 'Whether that be preserving a threatened environmental area or revealing the horrors of deprivation.'

'There are restrictions imposed on women photographers?'

It was a fact which irked her unbearably.

'Unfortunately feminism and equality in the workforce haven't acquired universal recognition.'

'Have you not once considered what your fate might have been if it had been you, and not your brother, who had taken a miscalculated risk and landed in the hands of political dissidents?' Shalef bin Youssef Al-Sayed queried with dangerous softness as he finished his drink and placed the glass down on a nearby side-table.

Topaz-gold chips glowed deep in her eyes as she subjected him to the full force of a hateful glare. A hand lifted and smoothed a drifting tendril of hair behind one ear. 'Shane refused to allow me to accompany him.'

'Something for which you should be eternally grateful,' he stated hardly.

Kristi caught the slight tightening of facial muscles that transformed his features into a hard mask. Impenetrable, she observed, together with a hint of autocratic arrogance that was undoubtedly attributable to his paternal forebears, and which added an element of ruthlessness to his demeanour.

'It would appear that, although a fool, your brother is not totally stupid.'

'Don't you dare—'

She halted mid-sentence as Rochelle entered the room unannounced. 'Hilary is ready to serve dinner.'

Shalef bin Youssef Al-Sayed nodded briefly, and Rochelle exited as soundlessly as she had appeared.

'You were saying?'

'You have no reason to insult my brother,' she asserted fiercely.

He smiled, although it didn't reach his eyes. 'Familial loyalty can sometimes appear blind.' He stood and moved towards her. 'Shall we go in to dinner?'

Kristi tried to bank down her resentment as she vacated the chair. 'I seem to have lost my appetite.'

'Perhaps you can attempt to find it.'

CHAPTER THREE

THE dining room was smaller than she'd imagined, although scarcely *small*, with its beautiful antique table and seating for eight, and a long chiffonier. Glassed cabinets housed an enviable collection of china and crystal. Expensive paintings and gilt-framed mirrors adorned the walls, and light from electric candles was reflected in an exquisite crystal chandelier. Several silver-domed covers dominated the table, with its centrepiece of exotic orchids.

Kristi slid into the chair that Shalef bin Youssef Al-Sayed held out for her, then he moved round to take a seat opposite.

A middle-aged woman with pleasant features busied herself removing covers from the heated platters, then indicated a choice of desserts and the cheeseboard, laid out atop the chiffonier.

With a cheerful smile, Hilary—it had to be Hilary, Kristi surmised—turned toward her employer. 'Shall I serve the soup?'

'Thank you, Hilary. We'll manage.'

'Ring when you require coffee.'

He removed the lid from a china tureen. 'I trust you enjoy leek and potato soup, Miss Dalton?'

'Yes.'

He took her plate and ladled out a medium portion before tending to his own. *'Bon appetit,'* he said with a tinge of mockery, and she inclined her head in silent acknowledgement.

The soup was delicious, and followed by superb beef Wellington with an assortment of vegetables.

'Wine?'

'Just a little,' Kristi agreed, motioning for him to stop when the glass was half-filled.

He ate with an economy of movement, his hands broad, with a sprinkling of dark hair, the fingers long, well formed and obviously strong. She could imagine them reining in a horse and manoeuvring the wheel of a rugged four-wheel drive. Gently drifting over the skin of a responsive woman. *Hell,* where did that come from? Her hand paused midway to her mouth, then she carefully returned the fork to rest on her plate. The pressure of the past few weeks, culminating over the last two days, had finally taken its toll. She was going insane. There seemed no other logical explanation for the passage of her thoughts.

'Can I help you to some more vegetables?'

Her vision cleared, and she swallowed in an endeavour to ease the constriction in her throat. 'No. Thank you,' she added in a voice that sounded slightly husky.

He had eaten more quickly than she, consuming twice the amount of food.

'Dessert?'

She settled for some fresh fruit, and followed it with a sliver of brie, observing his choice of apple crumble with cream. The man had a sweet tooth. Somehow it made him seem more human.

'Shall we return to the lounge for coffee?'

'Thank you,' she returned politely, watching as he dispensed with his napkin. Kristi did likewise and then stood.

He moved to the door and opened it, ushering her into the hallway.

A host of butterfly wings began to flutter inside her stomach. The past two hours had been devoted to observing the conventions. Now it was down to business. And somehow she had to convince him that she'd use the information she held against him in order to ensure that he would enlist Mehmet Hassan's help in freeing her brother.

'Make yourself comfortable,' Shalef bin Youssef Al-Sayed bade her as they entered the lounge, and she watched as he pressed an electronic button beside the wall-switch. 'Hilary will bring coffee.'

Kristi sank into the same chair she'd occupied on her arrival. 'Sheikh bin Al-Sayed.' Now that the moment had come, it was costing her more effort than she'd envisaged. 'Dinner was very pleasant,' she began. 'But now—'

'You want to discuss business,' he concluded with a touch of mockery as he took the chair opposite. 'Yes.'

He placed an elbow on each arm of the chair and steepled his fingers, assuming an enigmatic expression that she couldn't begin to fathom. 'The ball is in your court, Miss Dalton. I suggest you play it.'

Her eyes were steady, the tip of her chin tilting at a firm angle as she carefully put the metaphorical ball in motion. 'When do you plan leaving for Riyadh?'

'Next week.'

The butterfly wings increased their tempo inside her stomach. 'With your influence I imagine that allows sufficient time to have the necessary sponsorship papers processed.'

'Indeed.'

So far, so good. 'Perhaps you could let me have flight details, and any relevant information I need.'

He was silent for several seconds, and the silence seemed to grow louder with each one that passed.

'The flight details are simple, Miss Dalton. We board a commercial airline to Bahrain, then take my private jet to Riyadh.' He regarded her with an intensity that had the butterfly wings beating a frantic tattoo. 'Not so simple is the reason for your accompanying me.'

It seemed such a small detail. 'Why?'

'My father's third wife and her two daughters live in the palace, each of whom will be wildly curious as to why I have chosen to bring a woman with me.'

Surprise widened her eyes. 'You're joking. Aren't you?' she queried doubtfully.

'Since I can avail myself of any woman I choose,' he drawled hatefully, 'the fact that I have brought one with me will be viewed as having considerable significance—not only by my late father's family, but by several of my friends.' He smiled—a mere facsimile which held an element of pitiless disregard. 'Tell me, Miss Dalton, would you prefer to be accepted as the woman in my life, or a—' he paused imperceptibly '—transitory attraction?'

Hilary chose that moment to enter the room, wheeling a trolley bearing a silver coffee-pot, two cups and saucers, milk, cream and sugar, together with a plate of petit fours.

'Thank you, Hilary. The meal was superb, as usual,' Shalef bin Youssef Al-Sayed complimented her while Kristi inwardly seethed with anger. Somehow she managed to dredge up a smile and add to her host's praise. However, the instant that Hilary disappeared out the door she launched into immediate attack.

'What is wrong with presenting me to your family as a guest?' she demanded heatedly.

His eyes hardened measurably, and she felt the beginnings of unease. 'I accord Nashwa and her two daughters the respect they deserve. Whenever I visit Riyadh I observe the customs of my father's country for the duration of my stay. As sponsor, I must vouch for your good behaviour while you are in Saudi Arabia, take responsibility for your welfare, and ensure your departure when it is time for you to leave.'

Kristi lifted a hand, then let it fall in a gesture of helpless anger. Her main consideration was Shane, and the influence that Shalef bin Youssef Al-Sayed could wield with Mehmet Hassan in negotiating her brother's release.

'OK,' she agreed. 'I don't particularly like the idea of pretending to be your woman but I'll go along with it.'

He made no comment. Instead, he rose to his feet and proceeded to pour dark, aromatic coffee into the two cups. 'Milk, cream, or a liqueur?'

'Black.' She helped herself to sugar, then sipped the strong brew, watching as he did likewise. When she finished she placed her cup and saucer down on a nearby table and stood up. 'If you could arrange a taxi for me, Sheikh bin Al-Sayed, I'd like to return to my hotel.'

'Shalef,' he corrected silkily. 'As we're to be linked together, it will be thought strange if you continue to address me with such formality.' He unfolded his lengthy frame with lithe ease. 'I'll drive you into the city.'

Why did that cause an immediate knot to form in her stomach? 'A taxi would be less inconvenient.'

'To whom?'

She looked at him carefully. 'To you, of course. An hour's drive each way seems unnecessary at this time of night.'

'There are several spare bedrooms, any one of which you would be welcome to use.'

The hint of mockery brought a fiery sparkle to her eyes. 'As long as you're aware it wouldn't be yours.'

One eyebrow slanted. 'I wasn't aware I implied it might be.'

She drew in a deep breath. 'I don't find verbal games in the least amusing.'

It was impossible to detect anything from his expression. 'I'll get your coat.'

Polite civility edged her voice. 'Thank you.'

In the car she sat in silence, grateful when he activated the stereo system and Mozart provided a soothing background that successfully eliminated the need for conversation.

He drove well, with considerably more speed than his chauffeur. Or had it been his bodyguard? The miles between Berkshire and London diminished quickly, although once they reached the inner city any attempt at swift passage was hampered by computer-controlled intersections and traffic.

Kristi sighted the entrance to her hotel and prepared to alight the instant that Shalef bin Youssef Al-Sayed brought the car to a halt.

'Thank you.' Her hand paused on the door-clasp as she turned towards him. It was difficult to fathom his expression. 'I imagine you'll be in touch with the flight time?'

'I have been invited to a formal dinner on Saturday evening. I'd like you to accompany me.'

'Why?' The single query slipped out unbidden, and his eyes hardened slightly.

'In less than a week you will meet members of my late father's family. It would be preferable if we are seen to share a rapport.'

'Does it matter?'

'I consider it does. Be ready at seven.'

She felt the stirrings of resentment. 'I don't like being given an order.'

'Are you usually so argumentative?'

'Only with people who refuse to respect my right to decline an invitation,' she responded coolly.

'Are you dismissing my request?' His voice was dangerously soft, and despite the car's heating system she felt suddenly cold.

'No,' she said quietly, 'merely stating that I prefer to be asked rather than told.' She activated the door clasp and stepped from the car, hearing the refined clunk as she carefully closed the door behind her; then she turned towards the main entrance and made her way into the foyer without a backward glance.

It wasn't until she was inside her suite that she allowed herself the luxury of releasing an angry exclamation.

Sheikh Shalef bin Youssef Al-Sayed was beginning to threaten her equilibrium in more ways than one. She didn't like it, any more than she liked him. Nor did she particularly like the idea of partnering him to a formal dinner party. Except she couldn't afford to anger him.

Not yet, a tiny imp inside her taunted with mischievous intent. Not yet.

'Formal' was particularly apt, Kristi reflected with idle interest as she scanned the room's occupants. Twenty-four people sat at the table, and were served cordon bleu courses by uniformed maids and offered finest vintage wines by impeccably suited waiters. Gold-rimmed bone china vied with gleaming silver and sparkling crystal, and the floral centrepieces were a work of art.

Expensive jewellery adorned the fingers of the female guests, and there was little doubt that their gowns were designer originals.

'Dessert, Miss Dalton? There is a choice of tiramisu, strawberry shortcake, or fresh fruit.'

Although each single course had comprised a small portion, she'd lost count of the courses served and was reluctant to accept yet another. She offered the waitress a faint smile. 'No, thank you.'

'You have no need to watch your figure.'

Kristi turned towards the man seated on her left and felt the distinct pressure of his knee against her own. Without any compunction she carefully angled the tip of her slender-heeled shoe to connect with his ankle. 'I doubt Shalef would appreciate your interest,' she ventured sweetly.

'Point taken,' he acknowledged with sardonic cynicism. 'Literally.'

Her smile held no sincerity. How much longer before they could leave the table and adjourn to the lounge?

'Try some of this cheese,' Shalef suggested smoothly as he speared a small segment onto a wafer then offered it to her. His eyes were dark, their expression enigmatic, and her own widened marginally at the studied intimacy of his action.

Kristi's mouth curved slightly in response as she sampled the wafer. 'Superb,' she acknowledged. She had never doubted that he was dangerous. When he set out to charm, he was positively lethal.

'Would you like some more?'

'No. Thanks,' she added.

'So polite.'

'Don't amuse yourself at my expense,' she warned in a silky undertone.

He considered her thoughtfully. 'Is that what you think I'm doing?'

'You're playing a game for the benefit of fellow guests who are intent on displaying a discreet interest in Sheikh Shalef bin Youssef Al-Sayed's latest companion.'

'What is it you particularly object to?' he queried musingly. 'Being a subject of interest, or labelled as my latest conquest?'

Her gaze was level. 'I have little control over the former, but as the latter doesn't apply I'd prefer it if you would decline from indicating an intimacy which doesn't exist.'

'You have a vivid and distorted imagination.'

'While you, Sheikh bin Al-Sayed,' she responded evenly, 'parry words with the skill of a master chess-player.'

A soft chuckle started at the back of his throat and emerged with a genuine humour that was reflected in the gleaming warmth of his eyes. 'Shalef,' he insisted quietly.

Kristi looked at him carefully. 'I imagine it is much too early to request that you take me back to the hotel?'

His mouth curved with slow indolence. 'Much too early.'

'In which case I shall attempt dazzling conversation with a fellow guest.'

'Alternatively, you could attempt to dazzle me.'

She picked up her glass and sipped the chilled water, then set it down carefully. 'Don't you tire of women who strive to capture your attention?'

'It depends on the woman,' he said mockingly. 'And whether it's more than my attention she attempts to capture.'

The request for guests to adjourn to the lounge was timely, and Kristi rose to her feet with relief, glad of the opportunity to escape the close proximity of Shalef bin Youssef Al-Sayed.

But her freedom was short-lived as he moved to her side, and she didn't pull away when he caught her elbow in a light clasp as they made their way from the dining room.

Her senses seemed more acute, and she was conscious of his clean male smell mingling with the subtle tang of his cologne. His touch brought an awareness of sexual alchemy together with a heightened degree of sensuality that quickened her pulse and had the strangest effect on her breathing.

Such feelings were a complication she couldn't afford, and she deliberately sought to impose a measure of control.

'Shalef, how wonderful to see you again.'

Kristi heard the distinct purr in the light, feminine voice and glimpsed the perfection of scarlet-tipped fingers an instant before a model-slim, dark-haired young woman slid an arm through his.

Beauty enhanced by the skilful application of cosmetics and the clothes of a noted European couturier lent and exclusivity that was unmatched by any of the other female guests, and Kristi couldn't help the uncharitable thought that such a stunning result had probably taken the entire afternoon to achieve.

'Fayza.'

Was it her imagination or did she sense a barrier of reserve fall into place?

'Allow me to introduce Kristi Dalton. Fayza Al-Khaledi.'

The features were exquisitely composed, and her mouth curved into a smile that revealed perfectly even white teeth. But the brilliant dark eyes were as cold as an Arctic floe.

'If you'll excuse me, I'll fetch some coffee.' Kristi took longer than necessary in adding sugar and a touch of cream to the aromatic brew.

She started to show an interest in the mingling guests, assured her hostess that the coffee was fine and indulged in polite small talk. Not once did she glance towards Shalef bin Youssef Al-Sayed or the glamorous woman who had commandeered his attention.

'There was no need for you to desert me.'

She turned slightly as he rejoined her, and met his solemn gaze. 'Just as there was no need for me to compete.'

Shalef chose not to comment, and Kristi finished her coffee, refused a second cup and managed to contain her relief when he indicated that they would leave.

'You found the evening boring?'

The illuminated clock on the dashboard revealed

that it was after midnight, and she sank back against the deep-cushioned seat as the large car gained the motorway and gathered speed.

'Not at all,' Kristi assured him with polite civility. 'The food was superb, and one would have to grant that the company was equally so.'

'Including the guest who indulged in a surreptitious play for your attention during the main course?'

'You noticed.'

'He has a certain reputation,' Shalef informed her drily.

'I don't need a protector.'

'In London you can rely on Sir Alexander Harrington for friendship and support. In Riyadh it will be different.'

She turned to look at him in the semi-darkness of the car, noting the harsh angles and planes of his profile. 'Are you issuing a subtle warning?'

'A suggestion that you accept the political and religious dictates of my father's country,' he corrected.

'I won't attempt to wield any Western influence or encourage the younger members of your family to challenge your will, Sheikh bin Al-Sayed,' Kristi said with a touch of mockery.

'Shalef.' His voice was silky soft, and her stomach began to knot with nerves as she focused her attention on the scene beyond the windscreen.

It had begun to snow—light flakes that settled with an eerie whiteness on tree branches and hedges.

City lights appeared in the distance, and soon they were traversing inner suburbia at a reduced speed. Streetlights gave out a regimented glow, and most of the houses were shrouded in darkness, their occupants tucked up warmly in bed.

Kristi shivered despite the car's heating. In a few days she would board a plane in the company of a man she hardly knew, forced to place not only herself but the fate of her brother in his hands.

How long would the rescue mission take? It *had* to be successful. She couldn't, *wouldn't* contemplate failure.

The car eased to a halt outside the hotel's main entrance, and she turned towards the man behind the wheel.

'What time shall I meet you at the airport?'

He shifted in his seat and leaned an arm against the wheel. 'My chauffeur will collect you from the hotel. I will have you notified of the time.'

'Thank you.' She reached for the door-clasp and stepped out of the car. 'Goodnight.'

'Goodnight, Kristi.' His voice was a deep drawl that seemed to mock her long after she'd gained her suite and undressed for bed.

It kept her awake, then haunted her dreams as she slept.

CHAPTER FOUR

RIYADH rose from the desert like a high-tech oasis of glass, steel and concrete, with office towers, freeways, hotels, hospitals and, Shalef informed Kristi as his private jet landed and taxied down the runway, the largest airport in the world.

The subdued whine of the engines wound down to an electronic hum as the pilot wheeled the jet round towards an allotted bay. With almost simultaneous precision they slid to a halt as the hostess released the door and activated the steps for disembarkation.

Ten minutes later Kristi followed Shalef into the rear seat of a black stretch Mercedes. A man already occupied the opposite seat and Shalef effected an introduction.

'Fouad is the son of the daughter of my father's first wife,' he informed her quietly. 'He holds a managerial position with one of the family companies here.'

Kristi turned towards the man and inclined her head in silent acknowledgement. 'How many daughters are there?'

'Four. Two from my father's first wife, both of whom are older than me, and two younger, the daughters of my father's third wife.'

'Happy families,' she quipped lightly. 'I imagine there is a variety of distant aunts and cousins?'

'Several. My father's first wife developed cancer and died five years ago.'

The two men lapsed into Arabic as the large vehicle slipped free of the terminal traffic, and Kristi transferred her attention beyond the tinted windows.

This was a land where the muezzin called the faithful to prayer five times a day, where the male was revered while the female remained subservient.

She was intrigued by a culture that viewed women as less important than their male counterparts, their role so defined and protected that it amounted to almost total discrimination.

Did the women silently crave for more freedom, both in speech and action? To dispense with the *abaaya* and the veil, and adopt westernised apparel? And, if they did, would they dare speak of it to a stranger, albeit a stranger presented to them as Shalef bin Youssef Al-Sayed's current companion?

The Mercedes began to slow, and Kristi felt the nerves in her stomach awaken as it paused beside massive gates, cleared security, then swept through to a large courtyard.

The architecture was interesting—solid walls plastered in stark white, surprisingly small windows, given the hot climate, and an impressive set of carved wooden doors overlaid with ornate, metal-pressed panels.

One of the doors swung inwards as the Mercedes slid to a halt, and a middle-aged couple emerged to extend a greeting.

'Amani and Abdullah manage the house and staff,' Shalef informed her when he'd completed an introduction.

Indoors there was an assemblage of neatly attired staff waiting to greet their sheikh, and, although Shalef made no attempt at individual introductions, he presented her as a close friend from England.

The reception hall was the largest that Kristi had seen, with imposing marble columns and Carrara marble floors covered in part by a matched selection of exquisitely woven rugs. Tapestries adorned the walls, and expensive works of art vied with gilt-edged mirrors.

'At your request I have made ready the east suite for Miss Dalton,' Amani revealed. 'Refreshments are ready to be served in the sitting room.'

'Thank you. Shall we say half an hour?'

'I will take Miss Dalton to her room.'

Shalef inclined his head, then turned towards Kristi. 'I am sure you'll find everything to your satisfaction.'

Dismissal, she determined wryly. Yet she had expected no more. With a faint smile she turned and followed Amani towards a wide, curving staircase leading to an upper floor.

The palace was sufficiently substantial to house several families and still ensure individual privacy, she realised as she traversed a long, marble-tiled hallway.

Ornate side-tables and velvet-upholstered, gilt-framed chairs lined the walls and expensive silk rugs covered the marble floor.

'I'm sure you'll be very comfortable here, Miss Dalton. If there is anything you need, please don't hesitate to ask.'

Kristi preceded the manageress into a magnificent suite comprising sitting room, bedroom and *en suite* bathroom. The furnishings were an exotic blend of deep emerald, gold and white.

'Thank you.'

With twenty-five minutes in which to shower and change, Kristi managed it in less, choosing to use minimum make-up and leave her hair loose. Aware of a preference for women to wear clothes that covered their legs and arms, she'd packed smartly tailored, loose-fitting trousers, a variety of blouses and a few tunic-style tops.

As she added a spray of perfume to her wrists she couldn't help a wry smile, for the trousers and tunic top were a deep emerald...a perfect match for the suite's furnishings.

Would members of his family join them for refreshments? She had an intense curiosity to meet the woman who had been content to take second place to an existing wife. Had a sense of rivalry existed between the two women? And what of Shalef's mother? One could only wonder at her situation—an English rose, unversed in Islamic customs, set among the desert jewels. Yet if the

Prince had displayed his son's obvious attraction for the opposite sex it was probable that Shalef's mother had been caught up in a dream that had soon dissipated in the light of reality.

Kristi emerged from her suite to find a Filipino servant waiting to escort her down to the sitting room. It was a courtesy for which she was grateful, as the palace was vast, the rooms many, and she'd begun to wonder if she would need to embark on an adventure of seek and find.

They arrived downstairs and walked along a main corridor from which led three long hallways, linking, the servant informed her, further wings of the palace. No wonder there was such a large complement of staff!

The room Kristi was shown into was large and airy and filled with exquisite gilt-framed furniture, priceless items of gold-painted porcelain and original works of art.

Her eyes flew to the tall man who stood to one side of the window, his breadth of shoulder and stature emphasised by the silk-edged white *thobe* with Western-style collar and French cuffs. A white headscarf secured with an *agal* provided an electrifying effect, and made her all the more aware of the extent of his wealth, and his mantle of power.

'Kristi. Allow me to introduce you to Nashwa.'

She wrenched her eyes away from him and turned towards a slim, attractive woman attired in a royal blue traditional robe, whose dark hair was almost hidden by an exotic royal blue scarf beautifully embroidered in gold thread.

Kristi extended her hand in formal greeting, then followed Nashwa's action by touching her heart with the palm of her right hand.

The gesture brought forth a warm smile. 'I'm very pleased to meet you, Miss Dalton. May I call you Kristi?'

'Please.'

Nashwa's smile widened as she indicated a comfortable chair. 'Do sit down. Would you prefer coffee or something cool to drink? I can have tea served, if you wish.'

Kristi opted for coffee, then took a seat, all too aware that Shalef followed her action by choosing a chair close to her own.

'I understand you are a photographer. It must be an interesting profession.'

Kristi accepted a delicate cup and saucer from the maid, added sugar, then selected a pastry from an offered plate. 'My father founded a photographic studio, which my brother and I still operate. Shane's speciality is freelance photojournalism.' She smiled, unaware that her eyes held a tinge of warm humour which lent their hazel depths a velvety texture. 'He enjoys the challenge of venturing into far-flung territory in search of the unusual.'

'You have brought your camera with you?' Shalef enquired, his dark gaze steady, daring her to resort to any fabrication.

'It forms part of my luggage wherever I travel,' she managed evenly.

'I suggest you exercise caution whenever you use it, and request permission before you do.'

'Including the palace?'

'I would prefer it if you did not photograph any of the rooms within the palace. I have no objection to external shots, or those of the gardens.'

Security? She had no desire to flout his wishes.

She turned towards Nashwa. 'You have two daughters. I'm looking forward to meeting them.'

Nashwa's expression softened. 'Aisha and Hanan. They are aged twenty-one and nineteen respectively. Aisha is enjoying a sabbatical after lengthy university studies. Soon she will leave for Switzerland to spend a year in finishing school. Hanan is not quite so academically inclined, and after emerging from boarding-school in England at the end of last year she too has opted to join Aisha in Switzerland.' She proffered a warm smile. 'You will meet them both at dinner.'

Kristi sipped the coffee, finding it very pleasant if a little too strong, and declined anything further to eat.

Shalef, she noted, drank Arabic coffee flavoured with cardamom from a tiny handleless cup that was so small it looked ludicrous held between his fingers.

Nashwa was an impeccable hostess, adept at maintaining a flow of conversation, and Kristi found herself agreeing to a conducted tour of the palace itself, while Shalef retired to the study for a few hours in order to apprise himself of business affairs.

The palace was even larger than Kristi had imagined, with innumerable rooms set aside for the sole purpose of formal and informal entertaining. Opulent, she decided silently as she admired the elaborate draping. Each room was large, the colours employed lending a cool, spacious effect that was enhanced by ducted air-conditioning. An indoor swimming pool was Olympian in proportion, the tiled surrounding area sufficiently wide to harbour a variety of casual cushioned loungers and chairs. Beyond that were the Turkish baths and beautiful paved walkways meandering through an exotic garden.

There were three wings attached to the central building, Nashwa explained—one which she and her daughters used, one designated for Shalef's occupation whenever he was in Riyadh, and the remaining one kept for visiting family and guests. Staff were housed separately.

Encompassing two levels, the internal walls enclosed a central courtyard with lush gardens, palm trees and exotic plants. Numerous columns supported wide, covered verandas which could be reached from every room on the upper floor through arched doorways.

Kristi's tour was restricted to the guest wing and the entire ground level. Not offered were Shalef's quarters or those of Nashwa and her daughters. A dual purpose, perhaps...privacy as well as security?

'You have endured a long flight. Perhaps you would like to rest for a while?'

A flight that had been fraught with a degree of apprehension about the destination and its implications. Added to which, she'd been painfully aware of Shalef's presence and the vibrant energy he'd exuded as he'd relayed information about the history of his father's country, its rulers, and the positive effects of an oil-rich nation.

The thought of solitude for an hour or two sounded ideal. She could write a promised postcard to Annie, and Sir Alexander and Georgina would also value word of her safe arrival.

'Thank you.'

Nashwa inclined her head in polite acceptance. 'Dinner will be served at eight. I will send a servant to your room at seven-thirty, just in case you fall asleep. She will escort you down to the dining room.'

They were back in the reception hall and, with a warm smile, Kristi inclined her head before turning towards the staircase.

Her suite was delightfully cool, and she quickly discarded her outer clothes, then donned a silk wrap. An antique escritoire held paper, a variety of postcards, envelopes and pens.

Twenty minutes later Kristi placed the completed cards to one side, then crossed to the bed and lay down. Half an hour, she told herself as she closed her eyes.

But she must have dozed longer than she'd meant to, for she came awake at the sound of a light double tap against the outer door.

It couldn't be seventy-thirty already! But it was, and she flew to the door, opening it to discover a servant waiting outside.

'Could you come back in twenty minutes?'

'As you wish.'

Kristi closed the door and moved quickly into the bathroom, shedding her wrap and her underclothes, as she went. The shower succeeded in removing the last vestiges of tiredness, and she let the water run cold for ten seconds before turning off the taps.

She was ready with one minute to spare, dressed in long black silk evening trousers and matching top, her make-up understated except for her eyes. Jewellery was confined to a gold pendant and matching earrings, and she'd sprayed perfume to several pulse spots. There wasn't time to do anything other than stroke a brush through her hair.

The servant was patiently waiting when she opened the door, and Kristi attempted to dispel a faint fluttering of nerves as they descended the staircase.

'Dining room' was a slight misnomer, she discovered on being directed to a semi-formal lounge with an adjoining dining room.

Shalef was an impressive figure in a royal blue *thobe* edged with silver, and the butterfly wings inside her stomach beat a faint tattoo as he crossed the room to greet her.

'I hope I haven't kept you waiting.' Her voice sounded faintly husky even to her own ears, and her eyes widened fractionally at his indulgent smile.

'Not at all.' He caught hold of her hand and lifted it to his lips, his eyes silently challenging hers as he glimpsed her inner battle to retain a measure of composure.

He was initiating a deliberate strategy, alluding to a relationship which didn't exist merely to qualify her presence here. Yet Kristi had the distinct feeling that he intended to derive a certain degree of diabolical pleasure from the exercise, and it rankled unbearably that the only time she'd be able to castigate him verbally for his actions would be when they were alone.

Her eyes flashed a silent warning as she offered him a brilliant smile: Don't play games with me.

She saw one eyebrow lift in mocking amusement, and she had to marshal her features not to reflect the burning anger that simmered deep within her.

'Come and meet Nashwa's daughters,' Shalef bade her smoothly as he turned and led her into the centre of the room. 'Aisha.' He indicated a slim girl of average height whose dark gaze was openly friendly, then the younger girl at her side. 'Hanan.'

Both girls were beautiful, with flawless complexions and dark, liquid brown eyes. Each wore traditional dress, Aisha in gold-embroidered aqua silk, while Hanan had opted for a soft blue. Their mother looked resplendent in deep emerald.

At least she provided a contrast in black, Kristi decided as she smiled and offered the girls a greeting. 'I've been looking forward to meeting you both.' She turned slightly and included the young man standing unobtrusively a short distance from Nashwa. 'Nashwa. Fouad.'

'Mother says you're a photographer,' Aisha said politely. 'It must be a fascinating occupation.'

'Most of the time it's routine,' Kristi acknowledged with a touch of wry humour.

'I am to study fashion design when I return from Switzerland,' Hanan declared. 'Shalef has given permission for me to begin in London. If I do well, he will allow me to study in Paris.'

Nashwa stood up. 'Shall we all go in to dinner?'

Shalef took a seat at the head of the table, and indicated that Kristi should occupy a chair close to him. An honour, she assumed, that merely endorsed her place as his latest 'companion'.

The food was excellent—hot, spicy lamb served with rice and beans, followed by a variety of sweets laden with dates and honey. There was a platter of succulent fresh fruit, and Kristi opted for some sliced melon and a few dates.

They were waited on by a number of Filipino servants, who stood inconspicuously in the background as each dish was served, then moved forward to remove plates and replace them with each subsequent course, and no sooner was a water glass empty than it was unobtrusively refilled.

'Is your photographic work confined to studio portraits?' Fouad queried politely.

Kristi set down her glass. 'Frequently, in between assignments.'

'Tell us something about these assignments. Are any of them dangerous?'

'Not really,' she answered lightly, deliberately meeting Shalef's hard gaze. 'The risk is minimal.'

Shalef's fingers toyed with the stem of his crystal goblet. 'Indeed?'

Kristi held his gaze without any difficulty at all. 'You hunt in the desert and attempt to master the falcon. Is that without risk?'

'Attempt' was perhaps not the wisest choice of word. There could be no doubt that Shalef bin Youssef Al-Sayed achieved success in everything he did, and to hint at anything less was almost an insult.

'Your concern for my safety warms my heart.'

'As does yours for me,' she responded, offering him a sweet smile.

His eyes gleamed darkly and one eyebrow slanted in silent amusement. 'When we've had coffee I'll show you the garden.'

She forced her smile to widen slightly, while silently threatening to do mild injury to certain of his male body parts if he dared anything more than a light clasp of her hand.

At the mention of coffee the servants moved forward to clear the dessert plates from the table, and Shalef rose to his feet, indicating the conclusion of the meal.

The partaking of coffee was leisurely, the conversation pleasant, and throughout the ensuing hour Kristi was supremely conscious of the tall man who chose to sit in a chair close to her own.

For a brief moment she almost considered declining when he suggested that they stroll through the illuminated gardens, and she glimpsed the hint of steel in those dark eyes and was aware that he knew the passage of her thoughts. Then she gave him a slow smile and stood up, offering no protest when he clasped her elbow as they left the room.

The warmth of the early evening was evident without the benefit of the palace's air-conditioning, and she surreptitiously lengthened her step in an effort to move further from his side—an action that was immediately thwarted as he captured her hand in a firm clasp that threatened to tighten should she attempt to wrench it from his grasp.

'What in the name of heaven do you think you're doing?' She kept her voice quiet, but he could hardly have failed to detect her anger.

'If we act as polite strangers it will raise questions about our relationship,' Shalef said smoothly.

'We don't have a relationship!'

'For the purposes of this visit we do,' he reminded her.

She turned slightly in the pale evening light and was unable to discern much from his features. 'I'm not in awe of your wealth or of you as a man,' Kristi declared in an undertone. The first was the truth, the latter an outright fabrication.

'No?'

Her eyes acquired a fiery sparkle at the faint mockery evident in his voice. 'If I didn't need your help, I'd leave and be grateful that I never had to see you again.'

'But you do need me,' Shalef pointed out silkily. 'So we shall walk and admire the garden, and appear to be as engrossed in each other as the situation demands.'

A slight breeze riffled the palm fronds and teased the length of her hair. 'Perhaps you'd care to introduce a subject of conversation that we can both pursue?' she said.

'One that won't digress into an argument?'

'You could tell me how you coped when your father first brought you here.'

'Fill in the blanks that have not been written up in the tabloid press?'

'Alternatively, there's Riyadh itself. Islam.'

'Religion and politics are a dangerous mix,' Shalef dismissed.

'They form an important part of life. Especially in the land of the Prophet Mohammed.'

'And if I were to present you with my views what guarantee would I have that they wouldn't be written up and sold to the media?' he said drily.

She looked at him carefully, aware of the caution he felt constrained to exercise with everyone he met. A man in his position would have many social acquaintances, numerous business associates, but few friends in whose company he could totally relax. 'Is that why you retreat here several times a year?'

The gardens were extensive, with carefully tended lawns, shrubs, and an ornamental fountain strategically placed to provide a central focus. Water cascaded over three levels, and at night, beneath illumination, it was nothing less than spectacular.

No doubt for him the palace represented a welcome and familiar sanctuary, whereas she found that it contained an air of Eastern mystery that she wanted to explore. The people, the culture, their beliefs, the vast, definitive division between men and women. To read and be aware of factual reporting was not the same as experiencing it for oneself.

'This is the land of my father,' Shalef began slowly. 'A land where the power of nature can move tonnes of sand for no apparent reason other than to reassemble a shifting terrain. Man has plumbed its depths and channelled the riches, reaping enormous rewards.'

'Yet you choose not to live here.'

He smiled faintly. 'I have homes in many capital cities around the world, and reside for a short time in several.'

'When do you plan on going to the hunting lodge?'

He paused and turned to face her. 'In a few days, when the first of my guests arrive. Meantime, I will ensure that you see some of the sights Riyadh has to offer, such as the museum, Dir'aiyah, the Souk Al-Bathaa. Fouad will continue to see that you are entertained in my absence.'

His features hardened fractionally. 'I must impress on you the fact that as a woman you cannot venture anywhere beyond the palace unless accompanied by Fouad or myself. Is that understood? Women are not permitted anywhere on their own, and cannot use public transport. To do so will result in arrest. Nashwa will provide you with an *abaaya* to wear whenever you leave the palace.'

Kristi made no protest. Despite her personal views on such issues there was nothing to be gained by flouting Saudi Arabian religious dictates. 'Have we been out here sufficiently long, do you think?'

'You have grown tired of my company?'

What could she say? That he unsettled her more than any man she'd ever met? 'I think you're enjoying the pursuit of this particular game,' she ventured, meeting his gaze.

'There are advantages,' Shalef drawled.

'Such as?'

'This.' His hands caught her close as his head lowered and his mouth closed over hers, his tongue a provocative instrument as he explored the delicate interior and wrought havoc with her senses. At her soft intake of breath his mouth hardened, staking a possession with such mastery that it took considerable will-power not to give in to sensation and kiss him back.

When he released her she stood, momentarily bemused, then reality returned, and with it a measure of anger.

'That was unnecessary!'

'But enjoyable, don't you agree?'

She wanted to hit him, and her fist clenched as she summoned a measure of restraint. 'You're despicable.'

'Come,' he bade her easily. 'We'll explore the garden further then return indoors. By that time your anger will have cooled.'

'Don't bet on it,' she returned inelegantly, unsure just how much control she could exert during her sojourn in the desert. Shalef bin Youssef Al-Sayed was a law unto himself, but when it came to a clash of wills she intended to do battle.

Shalef was as good as his word, and during the ensuing few days he assumed the role of perfect host. In the company of Nashwa, with a Filipino chauffeur at the wheel of the Mercedes, he ensured that Kristi saw many of the sights Riyadh had to offer. They visited the museum, the Masmak Fortress and the Murabba Palace, followed by the King Faisal Centre for Research and Islamic Studies. There was also the King Saud University Museum, and Kristi displayed a genuine interest as their assigned guide explained the history attached to each of the finds from the university's archaeological digs at Al-Fao and Rabdhah. The Souk Al-Bathaa, Shalef explained as they explored what remained of it, had become a victim of Riyadh's rush into the twentieth century.

Being in Shalef's company almost constantly had a disturbing effect on Kristi's composure, as he meant it to have. His behaviour was impeccable, although she was acutely aware of the intensity of his gaze as it lingered on her a trifle longer than was necessary, the touch of his hand when he directed her attention to something of interest, the moment he caught hold of her arm when she almost tripped over the hem of her borrowed *abaaya*.

Frequently she found her gaze straying to the firm lines of his mouth . . . and remembered what it felt like to have it move over her own.

Kristi didn't know whether to feel relieved or dismayed when one evening he suggested that they dine together in town.

'The night-life here is notoriously thin,' Shalef revealed, watching the fleeting play of emotions on her expressive features. 'However, the hotels have excellent restaurants, and the Al-Khozama has one I can recommend.'

With Nashwa and Fouad present, there wasn't much she could do but agree.

The *abaaya* was a necessary addition, but beneath it she wore silk evening trousers and a camisole top, and kept her make-up to a minimum. In some ways it had been amusing to discover that Nashwa, Aisha and Hanan each wore modern Western clothes beneath their *abaayas*. Saudi Arabian women, they assured her, spent a fortune on European couture.

Shalef was accorded due deference at the hotel as the *maître d'* escorted them to a table reserved, Kristi surmised, for the privileged few.

Choosing mineral water, she deliberated over the choice of starter and main course, conferred with Shalef and was guided by his selection.

'When do you leave for the hunting lodge?'

'Tomorrow.'

At last, she breathed silently with a sense of relief. There were questions she wanted to ask, but refrained from putting them into words, choosing to wonder in silence when Mehmet Hassan would arrive, and how soon it would be before negotiations for Shane's release could be initiated.

'How long will you be away?'

Their drinks arrived and it was a few minutes before he answered.

'A week.'

'I can only wish you an enjoyable and successful sojourn with your guests.'

He inclined his head in mocking acknowledgement. 'While you will be glad to be free of my presence.'

'Of course,' she agreed sweetly. 'It will be a relief not to have to pretend to be enamoured of you.'

The starter was served and Kristi found it delectable. The main course, when it arrived, was a visual work of art.

'It seems a shame to disturb such artistic symmetry.' She picked up her fork and carefully speared a segment of lamb, then paused in the action of transferring it to her mouth as a waiter approached the table and spoke to Shalef in a respectful undertone, listened to the response, then bowed his head and moved away.

'Fayza is visiting her family in Riyadh,' Shalef revealed. 'She is here with her brother and suggests we join them for coffee. Do you mind?'

Oh, *joy*. 'Why not?' Her smile was bright, her tone vivacious.

'You're in danger of creating a case of overkill,' he drawled.

'Why, *Shalef*,' she reproved with deliberate mockery, 'would I do such a thing?'

His eyes gleamed with dark humour. 'I suspect you might.'

'We could,' Kristi mused thoughtfully, 'consider it pay-back time for your unwarranted kiss in the garden.'

One eyebrow rose. 'Unwarranted?'

'Finish your dinner,' she bade him solemnly. 'We mustn't keep the lovely Fayza waiting.'

'Remind me to exact due punishment.'

'A threat?'

'More in the nature of a promise.'

She pretended deliberation. 'Is she merely one of many women in your life or is she special?'

'I have known Fayza for a number of years.'

'Ah,' Kristi responded with comprehension, 'the "we're just good friends" spiel. Does she know that?' She looked at him, then shook her head. 'No, don't answer. She lusts after you, and your wealth is a magnificent bonus. Or should it be the other way round?' She savoured another mouthful of food. 'Mmm, this is good.' She summoned a winsome smile. 'Should I play the jealous "companion", do you think? Take your hands off him, he's mine? Or the bored socialite who knows she has you by the ... Well, let's just say I'm very sure I have your attention.'

Shalef finished the course and replaced his cutlery. 'One day some man is going to take you severely in hand.'

'Rest assured it won't be you,' Kristi responded, pushing her empty plate to one side. 'Shall we enter the battlefield?'

Fayza greeted Kristi with polite civility, proffered Shalef a stunning smile, and allowed her brother to perform his own introduction.

You just had to admire Fayza's style, Kristi commended her silently almost an hour later. Demure, with a touch of the exotic, the hint of seething passion beneath a chaste exterior. Was Shalef fooled? Somehow she thought not.

'You are a professional photographer?' Fayza made it sound the lowest of lowly occupations, and Kristi had a difficult time remaining calm.

'It's a job,' she dismissed, and glimpsed the young woman's deliberate raising of one eyebrow.

'I have a degree in business management. But, of course, it's unnecessary for me to work.'

'What a shame,' Kristi sympathised. 'All that study and no need to apply it.'

Fayza's eyes darkened. 'Surely a woman's focus should be looking after a man? Ensuring his home is a tranquil haven?'

Oh, dear, what had she begun? Kristi wondered. She was in the wrong country, and probably in the wrong company, to converse on feminist issues. 'One has to allow that it's possible not all men desire tranquillity,' she opined with due cautiousness.

'Shalef,' Fayza appealed with just the right degree of helpless virtue, 'Miss Dalton has little understanding of a woman's role in Saudi Arabia.' She honed her weapons and aimed for the kill. 'However, I imagine such knowledge is of no importance to her.'

It was obvious that she was unsure of the precise depth of Kristi's relationship with Shalef bin Youssef Al-Sayed, despite the inevitable gossip which would have circulated among the cream of Riyadh society. It allowed Kristi the advantage of responding with an enigmatic smile.

'You're wrong,' she submitted quietly. 'On both counts.'

Fayza managed a creditable attempt at disbelief. 'Really?'

'If you'll excuse us?' Shalef asked Fayza and her brother. 'It's quite late.' He signalled to the *maître d'*, signed the proffered credit slip, then rose to his feet.

The fact that he took hold of Kristi's hand and enfolded it in his didn't escape Fayza's notice.

'One imagines you will fly out to the hunting lodge during your stay in Riyadh?'

Shalef's expression mirrored polite civility. 'It is something I allow time for whenever I am here.'

'Falconry sounds such a fascinating sport,' Kristi offered, and she gave him an adoring glance. 'Perhaps you could take me out to the lodge some time, darling? It would be a fascinating experience to witness your skill with the falcon.'

Shalef's fingers tightened measurably on her own, and there was little she could do to wrench them from his grasp as Fayza and her brother accompanied them to the hotel foyer, then stood briefly while the doorman summoned both cars to the main entrance.

Immediately Shalef and Kristi were seated the chauffeur eased the Mercedes onto the road and headed towards the palace.

'You excelled yourself tonight,' Shalef commented with dangerous smoothness, and she turned to look at him. The dim light inside the car accentuated the strong angles and planes of his facial bone structure.

'I wasn't the only one acting a part.'

'No,' he agreed as the car sped through the quiet city streets.

All too soon they reached the palace gates, and Kristi followed Shalef from the vehicle when it drew to a halt outside the main entrance.

'Thank you for a pleasant evening,' she said politely once they were indoors. 'Will I see you before you leave tomorrow?'

'The helicopter pilot has been instructed to be ready at seven.'

'In that case I'll wish you a pleasant stay and ask that you be in touch with any news.' She turned away only to come to a halt as a detaining hand clasped her shoulder and brought her back to face him.

'Don't,' he warned with threatening intent, 'concoct a scheme to visit the hunting lodge.'

Her eyes were wide and remarkably clear. 'Why would I do that?'

'You've dared many things in your career.' His hands crept up to cradle her head. 'The hunting lodge and the identities of my guests are *my* business. Do you understand?'

'Yes.' She *did* understand. Yet that didn't change her intention to put a carefully devised plan into action. For days she'd surreptitiously observed the servants' routine, and she knew where the keys to the vehicles were kept. She also knew how to disengage the palace alarm system, as well as the system connected to the garages. She had a map, and over the next few days she would encourage Fouad to enlighten her about the art of falconry and to disclose the precise whereabouts of the hunting lodge.

However, Shalef wasn't to know that.

'Make sure that you do,' he said hardly. His head descended and he took possession of her mouth, plundering it in a manner that bordered on the primitive, and when he released her she lifted a shaking hand to her bruised lips.

'I think I hate you.'

His eyes were so dark that they were almost black, and he offered no apology.

Without another word she turned and made her way to the wide, curved stairway that led to the upper floor, and in her room she slowly removed the borrowed *abaaya* and the silken evening clothes beneath it before entering the *en suite* bathroom. Minutes later she slid into bed and systematically went over every aspect of the palace security system, then mentally calculated when she would initiate her plan.

CHAPTER FIVE

KRISTI dressed quickly in blue cotton trousers and a matching cotton shirt, dispensed with make-up except for moisturising cream, twisted her hair on top of her head and secured it with pins, pulled on a cap, pushed her feet into trainers, then scrutinised her appearance, satisfied that she could easily pass for a reed-slim young man.

With a swift glance round the elegant suite, she caught up the backpack into which she'd pushed a change of clothes and minimum necessities then moved silently into the hallway.

The palace was quiet. In another hour Amani and Abdullah would begin organising the staff with daily chores,

Part of her deplored the subterfuge of removing the remote control and spare set of keys to the four-wheel drive from Abdullah's desk. It made her feel like a thief.

Kristi gained the ground floor and made her way to a rear side-door, disengaged the security alarm, then slipped outside and moved quickly to the garages.

For the first time she sent a prayer heavenward for expensive equipment as she depressed the remote control and saw one set of double doors lift upwards with scarcely more than an electronic whisper.

The four-wheel drive was large, with wide tyres and attached spotlights, spare petrol and water cans. There was no time for second thoughts, and she deactivated the alarm, then unlocked and opened the door.

She had driven a Jeep and a smaller four-wheel drive, but this was a monster by comparison. CB radio, car phone ... the interior was crammed with every conceivable extra imaginable.

Kristi checked the low reduction, ran through the gears, then started up the engine. All she had to do now was deactivate the security alarm at the gates, release them, and she was on her way.

There wasn't a hitch, and she gave thanks to heaven as she gained the road and moved the heavy vehicle swiftly through its numerous gears.

During the past few days she'd spent considerable time memorising streets, time and distance. At this early hour of the morning there was no other traffic to speak of, and her passage through the city was uneventful.

In another hour it would be light, and by then she'd be on the long road snaking into the desert.

She calculated that she had two hours, perhaps three, before her absence would be noticed. What she couldn't surmise was how Nashwa would react to her carefully penned note. Doubtless Abdullah would be consulted, and Fouad. There was always the possibility that she would reach the hunting lodge before anyone could notify Shalef.

His anger was something she preferred not to envisage, and a faint shiver feathered her skin at the prospect of weathering his wrath.

The buildings began to dwindle, the houses became fewer and far between, then there was nothing except the sparse expanse of desert, stretching out beneath the vehicle's powerful headlights.

Kristi seemed to have driven for ages before the sky began to lighten, dimming the shadows and bathing the land with a soft, ethereal glow. As the sun rose the colours deepened and the sky changed to the palest blue.

There was a sense of isolation—the grandeur of the sand and the gentle undulation of the land, the stark beauty of the contrasting colour between earth and sky.

The desert seemed so vast, so...inhibiting, Kristi mused. Frightening, she added, aware that a sudden sandstorm could cover the road, obliterating it entirely from view.

Don't even think about it, she chastised herself silently. It won't happen. And even if it did she would only be briefly stranded, for she could notify the palace—*anyone*—of her whereabouts via the car phone or CB.

As the sun rose higher in the sky its warmth began to penetrate the vehicle and Kristi switched on the air-conditioning and donned her sunglasses.

With careful manoeuvring she extracted a water bottle and a packet of sandwiches from her backpack, then ate as she drove, not wanting to stop and waste time.

As the sun rose further the bitumen began to shimmer with a reflective heat haze. It played havoc with her vision and brought the onset of a headache.

There was almost a sense of relief when she glimpsed a vehicle in her rear-view mirror. It gained on her steadily, then pulled out to pass.

There were two men in the front seat and the passenger gave her an intent look then turned to the driver. Instead of passing, they maintained an even pace with her vehicle, then gestured for her to pull over.

It didn't make sense, so she ignored the directive, accelerating to gain speed. Within seconds they were abreast of her once again, and this time there could be no mistaking their intention to have her pull over and stop.

When she didn't comply, the driver positioned the side of his vehicle against hers, and she felt the sickening thud of metal against metal.

She sped ahead, reached for the CB speaker, depressed the switch and spoke into it rapidly, giving her identity, approximate location and indicating the problem.

The men drew level again, and this time the four-wheel drive took a pounding. Kristi held onto the wheel for grim death and managed to get ahead of them.

Risking a quick glance in the rear-view mirror, she felt fear clutch hold of her stomach as she saw their vehicle in hot pursuit.

She was an experienced driver. With luck, skill and divine assistance, she thought she might manage to outdistance them.

Within a matter of seconds the vehicle was right behind her, then it pulled out and inched forward until it was abreast. The passenger gestured with a rifle for her to pull over.

There was no point in arguing with someone wielding a loaded firearm so she began to brake.

There was the sound of a shot, followed almost simultaneously by the soft thud of a blown-out tyre, then the vehicle slewed horribly to one side.

For what seemed like half a lifetime she battled to maintain some sort of control and bring the four-wheel drive to a halt, then she hit the door-locking mechanism, grabbed the car phone, hit a coded button, and when a heavily accented male voice answered she relayed an identical message, hoping, praying that whoever was on the other end of the line understood English. In desperation she repeated it in French before replacing the receiver.

She watched with mounting apprehension as one man crossed to the passenger side while the other attempted to wrench open the door closest to her.

They yelled instructions in Arabic, and shook their fists at her when she indicated a refusal to comply.

The man with the rifle crossed round to the passenger side, carefully took aim, then shot the lock.

There wasn't a flicker of emotion evident in their expressions as they gestured for her to move outside, the command enforced as the driver reached in and hauled her unceremoniously across the passenger seat and threw her down onto the ground.

Two hands grabbed her shoulders and dragged her to her feet. She stood still, returning their heated looks with angry intensity.

The driver reached out and pulled the cap from her head, then gaped in amazement and broke into a heated conversation with his fellow assailant.

Kristi lifted a shaky hand and tucked some of her hair behind one ear. The gesture was involuntary, and both men immediately stopped speaking.

Kristi fixed each of them with a scathing look, then pointed at her four-wheel drive. 'Sheikh Shalef bin Youssef Al-Sayed.' Then she touched a hand to her heart. 'Shalef bin Youssef Al-Sayed,' she repeated with soft vehemence.

The men conversed in rapid Arabic, arguing volubly for what seemed an age, then they turned towards her, subjecting her to a long look that encompassed her slim figure from head to toe before settling with stony-faced anger on her expressive features.

One word was uttered with such force that its explicitness couldn't fail to be universally understood.

It took considerable effort to hold their gazes, but she managed it, unwilling to respond in English, knowing that any verbal exchange would be totally useless.

The car phone rang, its insistent summons sounding loud in the surrounding stillness, and she lifted one eyebrow in silent query.

For several long seconds they seemed undecided as to whether she should answer, then the driver gave a brief nod and she scrambled into the front seat and snatched up the receiver. When she turned round the men were climbing into their vehicle, and, gunning the engine, tyres spinning, they roared at great speed down the road.

'Kristi? Fouad. Shalef is on his way. Are you all right?'

'I'm OK. The four-wheel drive hasn't fared so well.'

'And the two men?'

'They've just left.'

'Did you get the vehicle plate number?'

'It wasn't high on my list of priorities,' Kristi informed him drily. She thought that she detected a faint noise and quickly checked the rear-view mirror, then swung her attention to the road ahead. Nothing. The noise grew louder and her eyes caught a movement to her right. A helicopter. 'I think the cavalry is about to arrive.'

'The CB and car phone automatically access the palace,' Fouad revealed. 'The instant you rang in I notified Shalef on his mobile net.'

'I imagine all hell is about to break loose.'

'For me it already has.'

'None of this is your fault.'

'I am responsible in Shalef's absence. Therefore some of the blame falls on my head.'

The noise was incredibly loud, the rotor-blades whirling up the dust as the machine settled down a short distance away.

'I can't hear a thing. I'll have to hang up,' Kristi shouted into the receiver, then replaced it slowly as the helicopter door swung open and Shalef jumped down to the ground.

With a sense of detached fascination she watched as he strode towards the four-wheel drive. In a black *thobe* and red and white checked *gutra* he presented a formidable figure.

Suppressed rage emanated from his taut frame. She saw it reflected in his harshly set features as she wound down the window and sat waiting for him to say something—anything.

He opened the door and his eyes pierced hers, penetrating their mirrored depths. 'You are unharmed?'

Kristi wanted to laugh. Except that if she did, she'd never stop. Hysterical reaction, she recognised, and banked it down. This wasn't the first tight situation she'd been in, and it probably wouldn't be the last.

'I'm in one piece, as you can see,' she dismissed lightly.

'Then I suggest you get out of the vehicle.'

The four-wheel drive wasn't going anywhere in a hurry until some worthy soul jacked it up and changed the tyre.

With brief economy of movement she slid from the seat and stepped down. He was much too close, his height and breadth much too...intimidating, she decided.

'I'm sorry about this,' Kristi began, indicating the vehicle with a sweep of her hand.

'Shut up,' Shalef directed quietly, and her eyes widened fractionally.

'You're angry,' she said unnecessarily.

'Did you expect me not to be?' Hard words that had the power to flay the skin from her body. His eyes seemed to scar her soul. 'I issued express instructions that you were to stay at the palace.'

'I had a map,' she said.

'And resorted to subterfuge.'

'Fouad had nothing to do—'

'Fouad will answer to me. As you will.' His gaze raked her slim form, noting the graze on one wrist, the light scratch above her temple. 'The helicopter is waiting.'

'I have a backpack in the four-wheel drive.'

He gave her a searching look, then reached in and retrieved it from the floor. 'Let's go.'

Kristi walked at his side, protesting as he placed his hands at her waist and lifted her into the cabin.

'The rear seat. I'll take the front.'

It would have been difficult to do anything but comply, and, once seated, she secured the belt as Shalef swung up behind her.

The pilot set the helicopter in the air, then wheeled it away in a north-westerly direction. The noise precluded conversation, and since she wasn't offered a set of headphones she sat in silence and focused her attention on the swiftly passing ground below.

She saw the road, and three vehicles blocking another. Her assailants, surrounded by a party of men wielding rifles. Were they the police, or guards in Shalef's employ?

Kristi heard Shalef issue instructions in Arabic and the acknowledgement of the pilot as he swung away from the scene.

Were they heading back to the palace? She wanted to ask but dared not, aware that she would see soon enough.

Within minutes she caught sight of a building, and her breathing quickened as the helicopter cruised down to settle on a helipad inside the compound.

The hunting lodge.

The engine cut out and the rotors slowed as Shalef swung out onto the ground. Kristi followed, catching her breath as he lifted her from the cabin.

His eyes clashed with hers for an interminable few seconds, and she almost died when she saw the ruthlessness in their depths.

Retaining hold of her arm, he led her across a large grassed area to the house, and once indoors he traversed a hallway and drew her into a room near its end.

The door closed with a refined clunk, and the sound had an unsettling effect on her nerves.

'Now,' he intoned silkily, 'tell me everything that happened. Not,' he qualified, 'how you evaded the palace security system and commandeered one of my vehicles.' His eyes became faintly hooded, and she had the feeling that he was keeping a tight rein on his temper. 'From the moment you were threatened by those two thugs.'

Her chin lifted and her eyes were faintly clouded. 'What will happen to them?'

A muscle tensed at the edge of his jaw and his expression hardened with controlled anger. 'They will be dealt with, and charges laid against them. Most certainly they face jail.'

She shivered slightly, aware that the scenario could have had a very different ending if she had not been privileged with Shalef's protection.

'They probably wanted to alleviate their boredom by having a bit of fun.'

His hand slid up to cup her chin, lifting it so that she had to look at him. 'Saudi Arabian women are *not* permitted to drive,' he relayed with soft emphasis.

Kristi digested his implication in silence, unwilling to put a connotation she wasn't sure of on the two men's actions.

Her eyes widened as they searched his, and her stomach executed an emotional somersault that sent warning flares to various pulse spots throughout her body, activating a rapid beat that was clearly visible at the base of her throat.

'I'm sorry.'

'At this precise moment I find it difficult not to make you sorry for the day you were born,' he threatened softly.

Apprehension feathered a trail down the length of her spine as she willed herself to hold his gaze. 'Punishing me to appease your own anger will achieve nothing.'

He released her chin and thrust both hands into the pockets of his *thobe*. 'Your story, Kristi,' he reiterated hardly. 'All of it.'

With deliberate detachment she relayed what had happened from the moment the men's four-wheel drive had drawn alongside her.

Shalef listened intently, his eyes never leaving her face, and when she finished he turned and crossed to the window.

It probably wasn't the time to ask, but she had to know. 'Is Mehmet Hassan at the lodge?'

'No.'

Utter dejection dulled her eyes. Her trip to Riyadh had been in vain. 'So he didn't arrive,' she said in a flat voice.

'He flew out yesterday.'

'So he was here,' she breathed in sheer relief. 'Did you speak to him about Shane?'

Shalef turned towards her. 'There can be no guarantees,' he warned. 'None, you understand?'

Elation radiated through her body, turning her expressive features into something quite beautiful. 'It's the best chance Shane has.' Without thinking she crossed to his side and placed her lips against his cheek. 'Thank you.'

Something flickered in the depths of his eyes, then one hand slid to her nape, his fingers spreading beneath her hair to capture her head, while the other settled at the base of her spine.

Vibrant energy emanated from every pore, exuding an erotic power that she consciously fought against in an effort to retain a gram of sanity.

Kristi saw his head descend as if in slow motion, and her lips parted to voice an involuntary protest as his mouth closed over hers.

No man had ever kissed her with quite such a degree of restrained passion, and she shivered at the thought of what force might be unleashed if ever he allowed himself to lose control.

He plundered at will, ignoring the faint protesting groan that rose and died in her throat, and the ineffectual punches she aimed at his shoulders.

Kristi wasn't aware of precisely when the pressure changed, only that it did, and there was a wealth of mastery evident as his tongue explored the softness inside her mouth, then tangled with hers in a swirling dance that took hold of her conflicting emotions and tossed them high.

Almost of its own volition her body swayed into his, and her hands reached for his shoulders, then linked together behind his head.

His hand spread against her lower spine, lifting her in against him, and his mouth hardened in demanding possession.

The kiss frightened her, awakening sensations that tore at her control and ripped it to shreds. She wanted him, badly. So badly that when his hand moved to cup her breast she gave an indistinct groan of despair and closed her eyes, exulting in the moment and the heady emotions that he was able to arouse.

When his mouth left hers she made a slight murmur of protest, then cried out as he teased a trail of evocative kisses down the sensitised cord at the side of her neck. His lips circled the rapidly beating pulse as he savoured it with his tongue, and she went up in flames, uncaring at that precise moment as his fingers loosened the buttons on her blouse.

He dealt with the front fastening of her bra with adept ease, and she arched her throat as his lips sought one taut peak, tasting it gently, then teasing the engorged nipple with the edge of his teeth until she hovered between pleasure and pain.

Just as she thought that she could bear no more, he drew it in with his tongue and began to suckle shamelessly. Extreme ecstasy arrowed through her body, centring at the junction between her thighs, and she gave a low, gratified groan when his hand slid to ease the ache there.

It wasn't enough. It would never be enough. Yet when his fingers sought the zip-fastener of her jeans she stilled, caught between the heaven of discovering what it would be like to share with him the ultimate intimacy and the hell of knowing that if she did she'd never be the same again.

He sensed her indecision and moved his hand back to the base of her spine, trailing it gently up and down the vertebral column in a soothing motion that heightened her emotions even further.

With considerable care he closed the edges of her blouse and re-did the buttons, then he gently pushed her to arm's length.

'I'll instruct the servants to prepare something for you to eat.'

Kristi wanted to close her eyes and dismiss the previous ten minutes. Yet such a feat wasn't possible. Somehow she had to reassemble her emotions into some sort of order and act as if everything was normal. If *he* could, then so could she.

'I'm not hungry.' She had to look at him, and she managed it bravely.

'If you should change your mind, just go into the kitchen and help yourself.'

She didn't want to ask but the words tumbled out before she could halt them. 'When will you be back?'

'Before dark.'

He turned and left the room, and she could hear his footsteps retreating down the hallway.

Kristi stood where she was for a long time, then she stirred and looked round the room, noting the masculine appointments, the king-size bed. She walked to the *en suite* bathroom and examined the spa, deciding on a whim to fill it and take a leisurely bath.

Half an hour later she switched off the jets and climbed out, then towelled herself dry. She crossed into the bedroom and extracted fresh underwear from her bag, donned clean trousers and blouse, then went in search of the kitchen.

The lodge was reasonably large, comfortably furnished, and entirely male. Kristi wondered idly if Shalef ever brought any women here, then dismissed the idea. He had homes in capital cities all over the world. Why bring a woman here, when he could woo her in luxurious surroundings in an exotic location?

She found the kitchen and discovered it occupied by a middle-aged woman and a young girl. From the aroma permeating the air it was apparent that they were preparing a meal. Simultaneously they turned to look at her as she entered their domain.

The older woman beckoned as she crossed to a bank of cupboards, took out a plate and cutlery, then crossed to the stove and ladled a generous portion from each pot onto the plate.

It was more than Kristi could possibly eat, and she used sign language to indicate that she required less than half. Seconds later she was shown into an informal dining room and seated at the table.

The food was good, the meat tender and succulent, the vegetables cooked with herbs, lending a delicate flavour.

The afternoon seemed to drag, and she wished that she had something to read ... anything to pass the time. There was a television somewhere, for she'd seen a satellite dish when they'd flown in. Perhaps if she went on a tour of the lodge she'd eventually find it. There might even be stereo equipment and compact discs.

Kristi discovered both in an informal lounge adjoining the games room, and after checking the electronic remote control she switched on the television and went through numerous channel changes before settling on one.

It was after five when she heard the sound of vehicles returning, and she crossed to the window to watch as four men exited one Jeep and three stepped down from the other.

Shalef was easily identifiable, and she wondered which of the men were friends and which were staff. More importantly, did they speak English? If not, conversation over dinner was going to prove difficult.

From the sound of their voices it seemed that they'd had a successful day. There was deep laughter, followed shortly by the closing of doors as the men retired to their rooms to wash and change for the evening meal.

'I thought I might find you here.'

Kristi turned in surprise, for she hadn't heard Shalef enter the room. His black *thobe* had been exchanged for one of dark brown, and he presented an indomitable figure. A man who held sufficient power to shape his own life and change the lives of many of his fellow men. His effect on women didn't need qualification.

'You have a comprehensive audio-visual system,' she complimented lightly as she rose to her feet. His height was intimidating from a seated position, and she felt the need of any advantage she could gain.

He inclined his head in silent acknowledgement. 'Dinner will be served in half an hour.'

She looked at him carefully, noting the fine lines fanning out from the corners of his eyes, the vertical cleft slashing each cheek, and the strong jawline curving down to a determined chin.

Although she felt at ease in the company of men, she was aware of the segregation of the sexes in this country.

'It won't bother me if you'd prefer to dine alone with your guests.'

His eyes darkened fractionally and he made an impatient gesture. 'They know you are here, and I have no inclination to hide you away in a separate room.'

Kristi effected a slight shrug and cast her clothes a rueful glance. 'I'm not exactly dressed to impress.'

'You are not required to impress,' Shalef returned with mocking amusement. 'Shall we join our guests?'

The four men varied in age from early thirties to mid-fifties, and their status was evident in their distinguished bearing and demeanour. A Western woman in their midst was viewed with polite circumspection, and if they thought Shalef bin Youssef Al-Sayed had temporarily lost a measure of his sanity they were careful by word and action not to give a hint of this.

English was spoken throughout the evening, but although the conversation flowed easily Kristi gained the impression that her presence was an intrusion.

After coffee had been served she excused herself and bade the men goodnight.

In her room she shed her clothes, removed her bra and briefs, handwashed both and draped them over a towel stand in the *en suite* bathroom to dry, then she slid between the crisp, clean sheets of the king-size bed and switched off the lamp.

The darkness was like an enveloping blanket, and she lay staring sightlessly ahead, her mind active as she weighed Mehmet Hassan's influence in negotiating Shane's release.

How long would it take? Days—*weeks*? What if he wasn't successful at all?

Kristi plumped the pillow and turned on her side. She'd been up since an hour before dawn and she was tired.

Overtired, she cursed silently an age later. She should never have had coffee after her meal.

A shaft of light lanced through the darkness then disappeared, and she detected the almost silent click of the bedroom door.

Who—? She reached out and switched on the lamp, then gave a surprised gasp at the sight of Shalef in the process of removing his *thobe*.

CHAPTER SIX

'WHAT the hell are you doing here?' Kristi's voice was filled with outrage.

Shalef directed her a faintly mocking look. 'This happens to be my personal suite.'

She sat up, carrying the sheet with her. 'Either you go to another room or I will,' she vented with thinly veiled fury.

'The lodge has four guest suites,' he enlightened her. 'I have four guests.'

'Couldn't two of your guests share?'

'Each suite is identical to this one,' he revealed. 'To suggest sharing would constitute a grave insult.' His mouth curved into an amused smile. 'You are my...' he paused deliberately '...woman. Where else would you sleep, except with me?'

'Like hell,' Kristi said inelegantly.

'I don't perceive there is a problem. The bed is large.'

It might not be a problem for him, but there was no way she would calmly accept sharing the same room with him, let alone the same bed.

'I'll get dressed and go sleep on the sofa in the entertainment room,' she declared purposefully.

'And risk the possibility of being discovered by any one of my guests who might find it difficult to sleep and seeks the solace of music or television for an hour or two?' One eyebrow slanted. 'At least here you are beneath my protection.'

Anger lent her eyes a fiery sparkle. 'I don't want to be beneath you for *any* reason.'

He began to laugh softly. 'I'm pleased to hear you enjoy variety.'

Colour flooded her cheeks, and, without thinking, she caught up a nearby pillow and threw it at him, uncaring at that precise moment if he should choose some form of retribution.

He fielded it neatly and tossed it back onto the bed, then he continued undressing, and she was unable to look away from the superb musculature of his near-naked body. Sinews stretched and flexed, their fluid movement beneath silk-sheened skin a visual attestation to a man who took care to maintain a physical fitness regime.

When he reached his briefs she averted her gaze. She wasn't sufficiently bold to watch as he stripped off the last vestige of clothing.

Damn him. Didn't he possess a skerrick of modesty?

Determination set her features into an angry mask. 'I'll opt for the chair.'

Shalef walked calmly to the opposite side of the bed and slid in beneath the covers. 'As you please.'

'It doesn't please me at all,' she vented in a furious undertone as she scrambled to her feet. She wrenched the sheet from the bed and wrapped it round her slim form, holding it firmly above her breasts with taut fingers as she scooped up the excess length.

'Be careful you don't trip,' came a lazy drawl, and she turned to shoot him a fulminating glare.

The chair was large and looked reasonably comfortable, and she curled into its cushioned depths, adjusting the sheet so that it covered every visible inch of her, then positioned her head on the armrest and closed her eyes.

The early-morning start coupled with the events of the day gradually overcame her resentment, and she drifted into a light doze, only to stir some hours later as the air temperature dropped several points. The sheet was no longer adequate against the coolness of the air-conditioning, and she carefully attempted to reassemble its folds so that it provided another layer of cover.

Half an hour later any thought of sleep was impossible. There had to be a store of blankets somewhere, but as she had no knowledge of where they might be there was no point in trying to search for them in the dark. That only left the clothes she'd discarded earlier.

With considerable care she sat up and attempted to orientate herself to her surroundings. The *en suite* bathroom had to be directly ahead, the bed to her left, and the door to her right. Therefore all she had to do was creep into the bathroom, reach for her clothes, don them, and creep back to the chair.

She dared not risk putting on a light, even had she been able to remember precisely where any one of several switches were located. And the room was dark. Not inky black, but sufficiently shrouded to make any movement in unfamiliar territory a bit of a hazard.

Kristi knew that she could handle the situation in one of two ways: carefully, so that she didn't make any noise and disturb the man sleeping in the nearby bed, or brazenly, by searching for the light switch and waking Shalef. Somehow *carefully* presented itself as the better option.

The sheet had to go. It would rustle with every move. Seconds later she eased out from the chair and trod slowly across the room. Four, six, eight, ten steps. The *en suite* bathroom's door should be a few more steps ahead to her left.

Except that when she reached for the knob she discovered the wall. It had to be further along. Inch by inch she moved to the left, then clenched her teeth as her toe made contact with a solid piece of furniture.

'Kristi?'

She spun towards the sound of that deep male voice and cried out in anguished despair, 'Don't turn on the light!' Dear God, this had to rank high on her list of embarrassing moments. 'The sheet is on the chair!'

'And you're afraid I might catch a glimpse of you *au naturel*?'

He was amused. Oh, how she'd like to wipe the smile from his face and delete the mockery from his voice! 'I was looking for my clothes.'

'I doubt you'll find them in my wardrobe.'

She drew in a deep breath. 'I left them in the *en suite* bathroom.'

'Your sense of direction leaves something to be desired,' Shalef informed her drily. 'The *en suite* is several feet to your left.'

Kristi wanted to throw something at him and, preferably, have it connect with a vulnerable part of his anatomy. 'Thank you,' she acknowledged with as much civility as she could muster, then gave an anguished cry as the room was illuminated. 'I asked you not to do that!' The fact that he had a view of her back didn't make it any less mortifying.

'I doubt I could forgive himself if you were to add to your list of existing injuries.' She detected the soft sound of bedclothes, sensed rather than heard him move.

She began to shake, partly with anger, partly from sheer reaction. 'At least have the decency to get me a shirt—*anything*.'

He hadn't touched her, but she felt the loss of his immediate presence as much as if she'd been in his embrace.

Seconds later he was back. 'Lift your arms.'

She obeyed, feeling the coolness of fine cotton on her skin as he slid the sleeves in place, then smoothed the shirt over her shoulders. Her fingers clutched the front edges and drew them together.

'You look like a child playing with grown-up clothes,' Shalef commented with a soft laugh. The shirt-tail brushed the backs of her calves and the sleeves were far too long. 'Now,' he ordered quietly, 'get into bed before I put you there.'

She turned round to face him, increasingly aware of his essential maleness, and her heart leapt, then thudded into a quickened beat.

One eyebrow lifted in a gesture of silent mockery. 'Do you really want to suffer a loss of dignity?'

What price defeat? Yet she refused to concede easily. 'Don't close your eyes, Shalef,' she warned. 'I might seek vengeance in the night.'

He reached out and caught hold of her chin between thumb and forefinger. 'Be aware that such an action will have only one ending.'

Something clawed at her innermost being, tightening into a deep, shooting pain that radiated from her feminine core. Sex with this man, simply as an assuagement of anger, would tear her emotions to shreds.

'I don't like being manipulated.' Yet she was helpless in this present situation, and she hated the thought of capitulation.

'You placed your fate in my hands when you left the sanctuary of the palace for the desert,' he reminded her, tilting her chin as he studied the conflict visible in her expressive features.

She opened her mouth to voice a protest, only to have it stilled by the placing of his finger over her lips.

Her eyes mirrored her inner anguish, and the pressure on her mouth eased. 'You could have sent me back. Why didn't you?'

The curve of his mouth deepened as it relaxed into a faint smile. 'Perhaps it pleases me to have you here.' His forefinger brushed over the contour of her lower lip, then travelled a similar path along the upper curve.

A deep shiver feathered its way down her spine at his action, and she consciously stilled the flood of warmth that invaded her veins.

'To share with you the stark beauty and the cruelty of a land that holds such an attraction for the men born to it.' His hand moved to cup her chin, while the other lifted and held fast her nape.

Kristi hated the sudden breathlessness that seemed to have taken control of her lungs. She had to stop this *now*. 'It's late, I'm tired, and I'd like to get some sleep.'

His faint smile was tinged with wry humour. 'So too would I.' He released her, and walked round to the opposite side of the bed. 'Get in, Kristi,' he ordered with dangerous softness as he slid in beneath the covers.

Something leapt inside her—anger, fear, *resentment* at his high-handedness. Yet instinct warned her not to voice it. The consequences of doing so hung like a palpable threat, and she had no intention of providing further provocation.

With extreme care she took the few steps to the bed, then lifted the covers and lay down as close to the edge of the mattress as possible.

Seconds later she felt the slight movement as he reached for the lamp switch, then the room was plunged into darkness.

Her body was the antithesis of relaxed, with every cell, every nerve acutely tuned to the presence of the man lying within touching distance. It was almost as if every part of her was silently reaching out to him, *aware* to such a degree that she ached with need.

Imagining what it would be like to have him caress each pleasure pulse, touch his lips to every part of her body was an unbearable torture. And that would be only the prelude to a concerto that she instinctively knew would be wildly passionate, its crescendo bringing such tumultuous joy that a woman might feel as if she'd died and gone to heaven.

Or was it simply a fallacy, a fantasy created by emotions so strong, so impossibly vivid that the reality could only be a disappointment by comparison?

Kristi assured herself that she didn't want to find out. You lie, a tiny voice taunted.

Dammit, *sleep*, she commanded herself silently with irritated frustration. In desperation she forced herself to breathe evenly in an attempt to slow the emotional pendulum.

She wasn't successful, and it seemed an age that she lay staring sightlessly at the ceiling, hating, *hating* the ease with which the man slept beside her.

Eventually she must have dozed, for when she woke the darkness of night had been replaced by an early-dawn light that filtered into the room, dispensing with shadows and providing colour where previously there had been none.

Slowly, carefully, she turned her head, only to find the bed empty, and a long, shuddering breath left her body as she stretched each limb in turn before rolling over onto her stomach. One more blissful hour, then she'd rise from the bed, shower and dress, before seeking some food and strong black coffee.

The next thing she knew was a hand on her shoulder and a deep male voice intoning, 'If you want to accompany me into the desert, you have fifteen minutes to dress and eat.'

Kristi lifted her head from the pillow and felt her pulse leap at the sight of Shalef standing at the side of the bed.

'I thought you had already left.' With deft movements she secured the top few buttons of her shirt, tugged its length into respectability, then slid to her feet.

'My guests have. I'll join them later in the day.' He reached out and smoothed back the tousled length of her hair.

The breath caught in her throat, momentarily robbing her of the ability to speak. 'Please don't do that.'

His smile was infinitely lazy. 'You sound almost afraid.'

Because I am, she longed to cry out. 'You said fifteen minutes,' she reminded him, neatly side-stepping him as she moved towards the *en suite* bathroom.

'I'll have one of the servants pour your coffee.'

She would have been willing to swear that she detected a tinge of humour in his voice, and she quickly showered, then pulled on her clothes.

When she entered the dining room there was a dish of fresh fruit salad, toast, and the tantalising aroma of freshly brewed coffee, steaming from a small pot.

When she had finished the meal she joined Shalef in the foyer.

'You'll need to wear a *shayla* and apply sunscreen.'

She stood perfectly still as he fixed the long scarf in position. 'Shall we leave?'

The four-wheel drive was the same model as the one she'd driven from the palace, and she wondered if he'd ordered them by the half-dozen.

An hour later Shalef eased the vehicle off the road and drove along a well-worn track for several kilometres before slowing to a halt close to a large black tent.

He indicated a tall elderly man moving forward to greet them. 'My father sprang from the seed of the Bedouin. I thought it might interest you to meet some of them. We'll be offered coffee, which if we refuse will cause offence. Remember to accept the cup with your right hand. Follow my example.'

He offered her a faintly quizzical smile. 'This man and his family have no command of English. They will accept your dutiful silence as a mark of respect for me.' He leaned forward and caught the edge of her *shayla*, adjusting it to form a partial veil. 'Let the edge fall when we are inside the tent and refreshments are about to be served.'

Kristi was enthralled by their hosts, and she was careful to follow Shalef's brief instructions, all the time aware of their circumspect appraisal.

Her jeans were well washed, their cut generous, and her chambray shirt was buttoned almost to the neck, the sleeves long and cuffed. The *shayla* felt a little strange, but it covered her head and shoulders.

Out here, she could almost sense Shalef's empathy with these people, the link by birth, the inheritance of definitive genes. He was at one with them, yet different.

His education, she knew, had been extensive, and gained in one of the best boarding-schools in England. He was fluent in several languages and held a doctorate. His business acumen and standing in the financial sector were legendary. Yet he spoke Arabic as if it were his first language, mingled with the Bedu, and chose the simplicity and the relative isolation of this desert land for his home for weeks on end at least twice a year.

Was the call of his Bedouin blood so strong? Or was it contrived out of duty to his late father, to Nashwa and her daughters?

The woman in his life would have to understand that, while she could be his hostess in London, New York, Paris, Lucerne or Rome, there would be times when she would need not only to accompany him to Riyadh, but to accept the severe restrictions that extended to women in this land. She would also have to don the *abaaya*, *shayla* and veil—light, gauzy colours in the palace, and black in public.

She would have to forgo her independence temporarily, and never in the presence of others would she be able to question his opinions, his direction or his wishes.

Yet there was a dignity, a sense of timelessness, an acceptance that was encapsulated in *inshallah* ... if God wills it.

Kristi watched as the coffee was served first to Shalef, then their host. Kristi was careful to accept her cup as Shalef had instructed, then she waited until he drank from his cup before attempting to touch the contents of her own.

She would have liked to know the topic of their conversation, but she sat quietly, instinctively aware that she should not intrude. When she was offered another coffee she didn't refuse.

The encampment was small, and there were a few camels that contrasted sharply with a Japanese-assembled pick-up truck. Even the equipment and utensils were at variance with each other. Water reposed in plastic containers instead of bags made from animal skins, and there was a modern transistor radio close to where their host's wife had prepared the coffee.

At last Shalef rose to his feet, his actions repeated by their host, and Kristi followed suit as it became apparent that they were preparing to leave.

Outside the tent, Shalef was drawn by his host towards the camels, and each was solemnly inspected and commented upon. Then came the formal farewell before Shalef made his way to the four-wheel drive.

As soon as they were on their way he asked, 'You found the encounter interesting?'

The four-wheel drive gathered speed, billowing dust behind it as Shalef headed for the bitumen road.

'Intriguing,' Kristi amended.

'Perhaps you'd care to elaborate?'

'You fit in so well, yet your Arabian persona is totally at variance with the Western image.'

'You find that strange?'

'No,' she said slowly. 'Somehow it suits you. Yet I can't help wondering if you suffer a conflict of interests. Having enjoyed the best of what the West has to offer, doesn't it even bother you that Aisha and Hanan are not free to experience the freedom of their Western sisters?'

He directed her a sharp glance. 'One does not choose the country of one's birth,' Shalef pointed out. 'One simply accepts the dictates of one's heritage until education and personal choice instil the will to change. Aisha and Hanan are fortunate in that their education will be completed abroad, they are free to work in their chosen careers, and they are free to marry—wisely, one hopes—a suitable man of their choosing.'

'Yet, as head of the palace, your opinion is sacrosanct.' It was a statement, not a query.

'Their welfare is very important to me. If they displayed bad judgement, and Nashwa requested me to intervene, I would hope to be able to persuade them to rethink the situation.'

'And if you failed?'

'I would take measures to ensure no mistakes were made.'

'Such as?'

'Refuse to hand over their passports, the restriction of their allowance.'

'Confine them to the palace?'

'The palace is hardly a jail,' Shalef reminded her.

She ventured soberly, 'It could be, if you didn't want to be there.'

'Since this is a purely hypothetical conversation, without any basis of fact, I suggest we change the subject.'

'That's a cop-out,' Kristi protested.

'A tactical sidestep,' Shalef amended.

'Because it's an issue you don't want to discuss?'

'An issue that cannot be addressed without understanding of the Koran in a country which has no constitution. Much of the legal system is based on a straight application of Islamic *sharia* law as interpreted by the Hanbali school of Islamic jurisprudence, the most conservative of Sunni Islam's four main legal schools.'

'I see.' It was a contemplative comment that brought a faint smile to his lips.

'I doubt that you do.'

She studied his features, wanting to dig beneath the surface and determine his personal views, rather than political observations. 'And you, Shalef? Do you consider yourself fortunate to enjoy the best of both worlds? The Western and Islamic? Or are you frequently caught between the two?'

'I accept my Arabian heritage, for that was my father's wish.'

'And when you marry, will you follow the Islamic tradition by taking more than one wife?'

'I would hope to choose a wife whose love for me would be such that there was no need to seek another.'

'But what of your love for her?'

'You doubt I could please a wife?'

He was amused, and it rankled. 'Sex is only one aspect of a marriage. There has to be mutual respect, emotional support,' she ventured. 'And love.'

'Many women would forgo the last three in exchange for wealth and social position.'

'You're a cynic,' Kristi reproved him, and caught the mockery evident in his expression.

'I have reason to be.'

She didn't doubt it. Women flocked to his side like moths dazzled by flame. Yet very few would be interested in the man himself, only what his wealth could provide in terms of jewellery and cash, magnificent homes and social prestige, in exchange for sexual favours.

The hunting lodge was clearly visible, and Kristi evinced surprise.

'Time flies when you're having fun,' Shalef commented, tongue-in-cheek, and she pulled a face at him.

'Lunch,' he announced in response. 'After which you can witness the taming of the falcons.'

'Birds held in captivity, manacled and chained,' she said with veiled mockery.

'Yet when set free they merely circle and eventually return to their master.' He swung the vehicle into the compound. 'They are well housed, well fed, and lead an infinitely better life than they would in the wild.'

'What a shame they can't communicate; they might tell a different story.'

He cut the engine and turned towards her. 'Then again, they may not.'

'You're a superb strategist,' Kristi commended him with intended irony. 'In the business arena you'd be a diabolical adversary.'

'In *any* arena,' Shalef corrected silkily, and she suppressed a faint shiver at the knowledge that there were few men, or women, who could best him.

CHAPTER SEVEN

LUNCH comprised grilled chicken, rice and a fava bean dish. The simple fare was filling, and Kristi accepted a small portion, preferring to complete the meal with fresh fruit.

'You wish to rest for an hour?'

She glanced across the table and met Shalef's steady gaze. 'You suggested showing me the falcons. I don't want to delay your joining your guests.'

'In that case we shall leave.' He rose from the table and Kristi did likewise, following him through the hallway to a rear door.

'The falcons are housed opposite the stables,' he indicated as they moved away from the house.

'You have horses?'

'Is that so surprising?'

Nothing about this man would surprise her. 'I didn't expect to find them here.'

'Do you ride?'

'Yes.' Her eyes glowed with remembered pleasure. 'I was taught as a child.' There was something magical about sharing the power rather than controlling it, the wonderful feeling of speed and the empathy one achieved between man and beast. 'They're beautiful animals.'

'Then you shall ride with me at sunrise tomorrow.'

A singularly sweet smile curved her generous mouth. It was months since she'd last ridden, and there could be little doubt that Shalef owned the finest Arabian stock. 'Thank you.'

'Is it the prospect of the ride or the sharing of it with me that affords you such pleasure?'

'The ride,' Kristi returned without hesitation, and heard his soft laughter.

The compound was large, much larger than it had appeared from the air, and she followed Shalef to the end of a long building some distance from the house.

'Stay there,' he bade her as they drew close to a large enclosure. 'You are a stranger, and the falcons will be wary.'

She watched as he unlocked an outer door and disappeared inside, only to emerge some minutes later wearing a heavy leather glove on one arm upon which rested a blue-grey falcon whose lower body was white with blackish-brown bars; it was leg-bound—attached to a short lead whose ring was firmly secured.

'This is one of my most prized falcons,' Shalef explained. 'It is extremely rare, and the most powerful of all the breeds. Its speed when it swoops on its prey is estimated at two hundred and ninety kilometres per hour.'

It looked fearsome, exuding a tremendous sense of predatory strength, and the claws, the beak were undeniably vicious.

'You enjoy the sport?'

'Falconry is a method of hunting game which was begun about four thousand years ago by the Persians. The challenge is in the training of the falcon, for it is an art that takes skill, a lot of time, and endless patience. First they must become used to having men around them. Then they are broken to the hood, which is placed over their head while they are carried in the field. The hood is removed only when the game is seen and the falcon is turned loose to pursue it. Finally, the birds must be trained to lure, so that they will not fly off with the game after they have struck it down or pounced on it.'

She looked at him carefully. 'One assumes you own some of the finest falcons in the country. Is that why Mehmet Hassan retreats here as your guest?'

'He is one of a chosen few.' The falcon rose up on its feet and arched its wings. Shalef said something briefly in Arabic and it immediately quietened. 'He's getting restless. I'll return him.'

Minutes later he rejoined her, and they walked slowly back to the house.

'You like being here.' It was a statement, and one he didn't refute.

'It's a place where I can relax and enjoy the company of valued friends without the intrusion of society.'

Kristi gestured towards the house, then widened the gesture to encompass the desert beyond. 'I can understand why. There is a harshness that challenges the survival of man.'

'Very profound, Kristi Dalton,' he lightly mocked as they entered the house.

Without thinking, she placed a hand on his arm. 'Thank you,' she said quietly.

'For what, precisely? Giving you a few hours of my time?'

'Yes. My being here must be a source of irritation.'

'Are you suggesting I deny it?'

She felt stung, the hurt incredibly strong for one brief second before she was able to mask it. She turned away, wanting only to be free of his disturbing presence, but a hand closed over her shoulder and forced her back to face him.

Kristi met his gaze and held it, hating him at that precise moment for being able to render her vulnerable.

When his head began to descend she averted her own, then she cried out as he cradled her nape so that she couldn't escape the pressure of his mouth.

She had no defence against a kiss that was hard and possessively demanding. He seemed to fill her mouth, exploring, coaxing a capitulation that she was loath to give.

Just as she thought she'd won, the pressure eased, and in its place was a soft, open-mouthed kiss that swamped her emotions and left her weak-willed and malleable.

The desire to kiss him back was impossible to deny, and her body swayed into his as she lifted her arms and linked her hands behind his head.

He permitted her to initiate a kiss, then he subjected her mouth to the explorative sweep of his tongue, teasing, tantalising in a manner that sent an electrifying awareness tingling through her veins, heightening her senses to a frightening degree as she began to melt beneath the magnetic thrill of his sensual onslaught.

Slowly, with infinite care, he eased the flare of passion, tempering it with one lingering kiss after the other on the soft fullness of her lower lip, the edge of her mouth, before trailing his lips up to rest against her temple. Then he gently pushed her to arm's length.

'I must leave.'

Kristi didn't feel capable of uttering so much as a word, yet she managed a sigh before turning away from him to seek the sanctuary and solitude of his bedroom.

A shower would rinse off the desert sand, and she'd shampoo her hair. Then she'd find pen and paper and compose a letter to Georgina Harrington. She'd also write a short note to Annie.

Thoughts of the studio brought forth an image of home. For a moment she almost wished that she were back in Australia. If it hadn't been for Shane, she wouldn't be in a desert a few hundred kilometres from Riyadh. Nor, she vowed silently as she stepped beneath the pulsing jet of warm water, would she be in a constant state of emotional turmoil over a man who could never be a part of her life. Or she a part of his.

*   *   *

It was late when the men returned, and after eight before dinner was served. Conversation was convivial, and it was clear that the falcons had performed well, the kill excellent. Kristi's vivid imagination conjured up their prey, the deadly power of the falcon, and she endeavoured to mask her distaste for a sport that centred on the death of the victim.

The last of the meal was cleared from the table and the men began to move into the lounge for coffee. Two of the guests displayed a penchant for strong cigars, and after an hour Kristi was conscious of a persistent headache as a result of passive smoking.

'If you don't mind, I'll retire for the night.' She stood, smiled at each of the men in turn, then moved towards the door.

Once clear of the room she contemplated taking a walk, but the evening air would not have cooled sufficiently for it to be more pleasant outdoors than in the air-conditioned interior of the house.

The bedroom was blissfully cool, and after brushing her teeth she undressed, donned the shirt that Shalef had provided the night before, then slipped beneath the covers of the large bed.

An hour later she was still awake and the pain in her head had intensified into a full, throbbing ache that showed no sign of dissipating.

Maybe there was some medication in the *en suite* bathroom that might alleviate the pain, she thought, and got up to see.

Switching on the light, she opened a drawer, and was in the process of searching the second when she heard Shalef's unmistakable drawl from the doorway.

'What are you looking for?'

'Paracetamol,' Kristi responded without preamble.

'Try the last cupboard above the vanity to your right.'

She moved towards the designated cupboard, extracted a slim packet, removed two tablets from the blister pack, found a glass and half filled it with water, then swallowed both tablets.

'You are unwell?'

She turned towards him. 'The cigar smoke gave me a headache.' Her fingers shook slightly as she closed the pack, and as she reached for the cupboard the pack slipped from her grasp.

She bent quickly to pick it up, then winced as the downward movement magnified the pain. In her hurry she neglected to foresee that the loosely buttoned shirt would gape, given its voluminous size, and she clutched the edges and held them tightly against her midriff. Her defensive action came too late, and there was little she could do to avoid the firm fingers which extricated her own from the cotton shirt.

'You are bruised.' He undid one button, then the one beneath it, drawing the edge down over her shoulder.

There were more bruises on various parts of her body, and he seemed intent on inspecting them all.

'You assured me you were uninjured,' Shalef said grimly, ignoring her efforts to remove his hands.

'I don't class a few bruises as *injuries*.' Her voice rose as his fingers probed a large, purpling patch close to her hip. *'Don't.'*

'You didn't suffer these from being held at bay, locked in the four-wheel drive,' he observed with deadly softness. 'Did the men undo the door and drag you out?'

His voice was like the finest silk being abraded by steel, and for some inexplicable reason her nerves felt as if they were stretched close to breaking-point.

'They didn't appear to understand English or French,' she related starkly, and the muscles of his jaw tensed with chilling hardness.

'Did they beat you? Touch you in any way?'

'They stopped when I said your name.' The words sounded stilted even to her own ears, and his eyes narrowed at the fleeting changes in her expression.

She watched in mesmerised fascination as he lifted a hand and brushed his fingers across her cheek then trailed them down to the corner of her mouth. Gently he outlined the contour of her lower lip, then slid down the column of her throat to trace a path over the stitched edge of the shirt to the valley between her breasts.

Then his head lowered to hers, and his lips followed an identical route as he pushed the shirt aside and brushed his mouth back and forth against each bruise in turn.

Something wild and untamed unfurled deep within her, flooding her being with a slow, sweet heat as his lips closed over hers in a kiss that was so erotically evocative that she never wanted it to end.

No man had ever wreaked such havoc with her emotions, nor made her feel so wickedly wanton as she returned his kiss and silently begged for more.

She needed to feel the touch of his skin, the silky external layer sheathing the finely honed muscles and sinews that bound his broad bone structure into a frame that was solely, uniquely *his*.

His clothes followed the path of her shirt, and she gave a silent gasp as he swept an arm beneath her knees and lifted her high against his chest to carry her into the bedroom.

The sheets felt deliciously cool as he laid her down on the bed; then he lowered his body beside her, bracing his weight with his hands as he began an erotic tasting path that slowly traversed every hollow, every intimate crevice until each separate nerve-end screamed for the release she craved.

Not content, he rolled onto his back and carried her with him so that she sat nestled in the cradle of his thighs.

Kristi stilled as he extracted prophylactic protection, broke the seal, then extended it in silent query. She accepted it with fingers that trembled slightly, unsure whether to feel relieved or dismayed. A bubble of silent hysteria threatened to escape her lips as she contemplated whether she could complete the task with any degree of finesse. Perhaps she could opt out and hand it back to him...

His fingers closed over hers, guiding them, and her discomfiture was no longer an issue as his hands slid to her shoulders and captured her head, forcing her mouth down to his as he initiated a long, slow kiss that heated her veins and heightened her emotions to fever-pitch.

The juncture of her thighs ached, and she almost cried out as he gently exposed the aperture then lowered her against the length of his shaft.

She gained some relief, but not enough, not nearly enough, and a low, guttural moan rose in her throat as he drew her forward and brushed his lips against the soft, aching curve of her breast.

His tongue sought one hardened, highly sensitised peak and outlined the dusky aureole, drawing it carefully into his mouth as he gently traced the delicate ridges, before teasing the peak with the edge of his teeth.

'Please ... Shalef.' She wasn't aware of uttering the plea, or that she said his name, and she gave a low groan of encouragement as he began to suckle. The pleasure was so intense that it became almost pain, and just as she thought that she could stand no more he diverted his attention to its twin.

His hands spanned her hips, encouraging a delicate sliding movement that almost drove her crazy, and she began to plead with him to ease the torturous ache deep within her.

He did, with such exquisite slowness that the alien invasion merely stretched silken tissues rather than tore them, and, when she gave a slight gasp and momentarily stilled, he stopped, sliding one hand up to cup her jaw as he forced her to look at him.

For long, timeless seconds his gaze raked her flushed features, searing through the moisture shimmering in those heavily dilated hazel eyes, disbelieving, yet having to believe, infinitely curious and filled with a white-hot rage that tightened the fingers at her jaw and sent his hand raking through the tousled length of her hair.

'You would set yourself up to experience the pain of vertical penetration,' he condemned in a dangerously silky voice moving fractionally so that she felt an edge of it, 'unsure whether or not you could accommodate me?'

She wanted to cry, but she was damned if she'd give in to a loss of control. A mixture of anger and despair began to replace passion, and with it came shame and a degree of embarrassment.

It was unnecessary to demand cessation, for he simply removed her, and she was unable to prevent an involuntary gasp at the acute sense of loss.

With an economy of movement he replaced the discarded covers, then settled back against the pillows.

She was incapable of saying so much as a word, although many chased incoherently through her brain. How could she tell him that no other man had made her feel the way he did? Or that there had been no one else because she'd never met a man with whom she'd wanted to share her body? Until now.

She lay quite still, consciously marshalling her breathing into a slow, measured pattern as she silently willed the tears to remain at bay.

They didn't, slowly welling and overflowing from the outer corners of her eyes, rolling down to disappear in her hair.

She wanted to slip out from the bed and dress, then leave the house and drive one of the vehicles through the night to the palace, where at first light she'd pack and have a taxi take her to the airport so that she could catch the first plane back to London. Except that she had no idea where the keys were, or how to neutralise the hunting lodge's security system.

'Why didn't you warn me?'

Kristi wasn't sure if her voice would emerge intact through the constriction in her throat, so she didn't even put it to the test.

The light from the bathroom cast a wide shaft of illumination across the bedroom, highlighting a strip of carpet, a large rosewood cabinet and a valet frame.

He shifted slightly, turning towards her, and even in the shadows he could determine a measure of her distress.

'If I had declared I'd never been this intimate with a man, you probably wouldn't have believed me,' she managed huskily. She'd led an active life, enjoyed numerous sporting pursuits. How could she have known her hymen was still intact?

'No,' Shalef admitted drily. 'Women usually choose to play the coquette, or pretend an innocence which doesn't exist.'

She didn't want to look at him, for she couldn't bear to see the mockery that she was sure must be evident, or glimpse the frustrated anger of a man who had pulled himself back from the brink of achieving sexual satisfaction.

She felt rather than saw his hand move, and she was unable to prevent the faint flinching of her facial muscles as he touched light fingers to her temple and discovered the damp trail of her drying tears.

She closed her eyes tightly as he followed their path, then slowly roamed her cheek with tactile gentleness, pausing at the edge of her mouth as he felt the trembling of her lips.

An arm curved over her waist and slipped beneath her shoulders as he drew her close, ignoring the stiffness of her body as he tucked her head beneath his chin.

Kristi felt his lips against her hair, and the light caress of his hand as he soothed the taut muscles in her back.

A rawness crawled deep inside her, an aching loss so intense that it was all she could do not to weep silently. She had come so close to an emotional catharsis that not attaining it generated a feeling of deprivation. And deep inside she experienced a measure of anger—with herself for being so blind in believing that her innocence didn't matter, and with him for calling a halt when, at that finite

moment, she would have welcomed the pain in
order to experience the pleasure she'd believed must
surely follow.

She lay very still, lulled by the solid beat of his
heart beneath her breast, and she closed her eyes,
wishing desperately for sleep to descend and blank
out the events of the past hour.

Part of her wanted a separate space, wanted to
turn away from him and move to the side of the
bed, yet the delicate tentacles of need were too
strong, the comfort he offered too pleasurable, so
she remained where she was, gradually relaxing until
the shadows deepened and she descended into a
dreamless state.

CHAPTER EIGHT

NOT quite dreamless, Kristi acknowledged from the depths of her subconscious as she ascended through the mists of sleep. She felt deliciously warm, and all her senses seemed to be finely tuned to the faint, musky smell of male skin beneath her lips. She could feel the soft brush of a hand as it trailed along her lower spine, while the other teased the softness of her breast.

Sensation unfurled as her body slowly wakened in response to his feather-light touch, and she murmured indistinctly as her breast burgeoned, its peak hardening in anticipation of the havoc his mouth could create.

She stirred, unable to remain still as the hand at the lower edge of her spine began to explore the contours of her hip, slipping down over her thigh to seek the core of her femininity. Her hastily indrawn breath was followed by a purr of pleasure, and her body arched against his as he began to tantalise her with leisurely expertise.

Every nerve-end began to pulsate until her whole body was consumed with a slow-burning fire that heated her veins and sent the blood pumping at an accelerated rate.

Slowly, with infinite care, he continued an evocative exploration of her body, heightening each sensual pleasure-spot to its ultimate pitch until she became suffused with an aching warmth. Not content with that, he repeated the exploration with the touch of his lips, creating such unbearable sensations that she clung to him unashamedly, silently begging for release from the tumultuous tide of emotion threatening to consume her.

Gently he eased himself between her legs, adjusting her hips as he coaxed her aroused flesh to accept his masculinity.

Kristi felt a sense of total enclosure as silken tissues expanded and stretched, and her faint gasp was caught as his mouth closed in possession over her own, the kiss so erotic that she didn't notice the sting of pain.

He began a gentle pacing, so that she felt every movement, every inch of the journcy as the music of passion built deep within her, its tempo increasing as she urged him further and faster in a crashing crescendo that culminated in shock waves shuddering through her body as she reached breathtaking ecstasy.

A total loss of control, she mused as she began the slow descent back to reality. Although reality would never be quite the same again.

Instinct relayed to her the fact that his response had been too controlled, almost as if he had kept a tight rein in order to ensure that she experienced the ultimate pleasure without threat of it being overshadowed by his own.

Awareness defined new dimensions, and she savoured the musky scent secreted by their skin, the warm heat generated by their bodies, their still rapidly beating hearts, his, her own, and felt them slow as languor replaced passion in the sweet aftermath of satisfactory sex.

Lovemaking, Kristi corrected silently. What they'd shared was more than just *sex*.

Slowly she turned her head, marvelling as the first light of the new day's dawn slowly crept up over the horizon, shifting shadows and bathing all before it in a soft, hazy glow.

'Do you want to ride out into the desert?'

The promise of a new day enthralled her, and she couldn't suppress the delight in her voice as she answered him. 'Yes.'

He buried his fingers deep in her hair, then bent his head and bestowed a brief, hard kiss on her mouth before moving to the side of the bed. 'How quickly can you dress?'

Kristi slid out to stand beside him. 'As quickly as you.'

Ten minutes later they were cantering out of the compound, the horses whickering slightly in anticipation of the exercise.

Her mount was a beautiful thoroughbred, with an arrogant head and a fine, pacing step that promised speed once she gave him the rein.

Shalef moved beside her, looking magnificent in traditional *thobe* and *gutra*.

The steed he'd chosen was large and powerful, and as soon as they cleared the compound he urged it into a steady canter.

It felt wonderful to ride again, to enjoy the exhilaration and the power. The terrain of the desert was stark, the sense of isolation intense, yet she could understand the fascination it held, for there was a sense of timelessness apparent, almost a feeling of awe for early civilisation. With a little imagination, one could almost picture the camel train of an ancient era traversing the distant sand-dunes highlighted against the early-morning sky, a caravan of wandering Bedouin seeking food and a temporary camp. And the marauding plunder of tribal bands who sought to gain and mark territory in a land which had known violence since the beginning of time.

A faint shiver ran down Kristi's spine, and in an attempt to dispel such introspection she leaned forward in the saddle and urged her mount to increase his speed. Faster, until every muscle in her body strained and the air rushed through her clothes, tearing at her headscarf and loosening her hair.

Shalef drew abreast and maintained an identical pace as they raced together across the wide plain without any sense of competition, until Kristi eased back slightly, allowing her mount to slow to a canter.

A hand reached out and caught hold of her reins, and she straightened in the saddle, her features alive as she turned towards the man whose thigh was almost brushing her own.

He wasn't even breathing heavily, while she needed precious seconds to gain control of her voice.

'That was incredible!' Her eyes were deep brown velvet specked with glowing topaz, and her cheeks held a blush-pink glow from exertion. The scarf had come adrift, and her hair was in a state of tousled disarray.

'So are you,' Shalef offered softly, and her eyes widened as he leaned close and took her mouth in a long, hard kiss.

It was after seven when they entered the compound, and as they drew close to the stables two Filipino servants emerged to take care of the horses.

'Would you prefer a cold drink or coffee?' Shalef enquired as they entered the house.

'Cold,' Kristi responded without hesitation, following him through to the kitchen.

'Water or orange juice?'

'Juice.' She ran a hand over the taut muscles of one arm. 'Then I'm going to have a long, hot shower.'

The cook looked up as they entered, moving quickly to the refrigerator to extract a carafe of orange juice and chilled water before she tended to the coffee.

Kristi was supremely conscious of the man at her side, and all her fine body hairs seemed to extend like tiny antennae in recognition of his proximity. All her senses appeared to be in a state of heightened anticipation, for she was conscious of every breath she took, every beat of her heart, and it bothered her more than she cared to admit.

The hand that held her glass felt slightly unsteady, and she drank quickly in the need to escape his disturbing presence.

In the bedroom she gathered her spare set of clothes, which seemed to disappear and reappear freshly laundered in a short space of time each morning, and went through to the bathroom.

It took only seconds to discard her jeans and blouse, briefs and bra, and for a moment she looked wistfully at the spa-bath, then decided on the shower.

Kristi moved the dial to 'WARM', stepped beneath the flow of water and picked up the bar of soap. 'Bliss,' she breathed minutes later as she applied shampoo to her hair, only to freeze at the sound of the shower door sliding open.

Shalef stood framed in the aperture, and her eyes flew to his in consternation.

'You can't,' she protested as he stepped in beside her and closed the door.

'I can.' Irrefutable, the words merely confirmed his action, and she gave a startled gasp when he removed the shampoo bottle from her hand and completed her task, massaging her scalp with tactile expertise as the water rinsed the suds from her hair.

The soap came next, and she swept his hand aside as it glided over one breast then moved towards the other. 'Don't.'

The remonstration brought forth a husky laugh. 'You are embarrassed? After what we shared together in the early hours of this morning?'

His hand moved to her abdomen, then traced across to her hip and slid to the base of her spine, soothing in a manner which tugged alive a fierce ache in the pit of her stomach.

'Shalef—'

Whatever else she might have uttered was lost as his mouth covered hers in a kiss that became flagrantly seductive as it gently coaxed, seeking a response that she was afraid to give. Her hands reached out, touching hard muscle and sinew as her fingers conducted a slow tracing of his ribcage, the indentation of his hard waist, and down over the flat musculature of his stomach.

A deep groan sounded low in his throat as he caught hold of her hands and held them, then his mouth eased away from hers and he rested his chin on the top of her head.

'Enough,' he said heavily. 'Otherwise we'll never get beyond the bedroom and there are guests who expect to sit down to breakfast with me in fifteen minutes.' He moved fractionally, letting his hand slide to cover her breast. 'Go.'

Kristi went, pausing only long enough to collect a towel, basic toiletries and her clothes.

By the time he entered the bedroom she was dressed and doing the best she could to persuade her damp hair into a semblance of order.

She was aware of his every move as he extracted briefs, trousers, shirt, and donned each of them before reaching for a clean *thobe*.

'Ready?'

Physically, although her emotions were in a questionable state!

The meal seemed to last for ever, the men inclined to linger over several cups of coffee, and it was almost ten when Shalef accompanied them out to the waiting helicopter.

The sound of the rotor-blades intensified, then the craft lifted off, paused, then wheeled away to the east.

Kristi listened till the sound disappeared, and she turned as Shalef re-entered the house. Her eyes locked with his as she tried to disguise her uncertainty. 'When do we leave for the palace?'

His expression was impossible to read. 'There is no immediate need to return for a few days.'

Kristi couldn't think of a thing to say.

'Unless, of course, you object,' Shalef added quietly.

She knew she should. Knew that to remain here with him was akin to divine madness. Yet the rational part of her brain was motivated by the dictates of her heart, urging her to embark on an emotional experience that would almost certainly end in heartbreak... although the journey itself would be unforgettable.

'I'll stay.'

Without a word he closed the distance between them and swept her into his arms.

'What do you think you're doing?' she asked in a faintly scandalised voice.

'Taking you to bed.' He carried her down the wide hallway to the room at its very end, then, once inside, he closed the door and allowed her to slide down to her feet.

Her eyes widened slightly at the vital vibrancy evident in those strong facial features, and she was unable to hide her own haunting vulnerability as his head began a slow descent.

The touch of his lips tantalised as they traced the outline of her mouth with evocative persuasion, then slid to the sensitive cord at the edge of her neck, grazing the sweet hollows before trailing up to take possession of her mouth.

Firm fingers dispensed with her clothes, then his own, and before she had time for coherent thought he urged her towards the bed and drew her onto its wide expanse.

Kristi lay still, mesmerised by her heightened senses and enraptured by the dark passion evident in his eyes. This close, she could sense the clean body smell emanating from his skin, and awareness coursed through her body like an igniting flame.

Her lips parted as he sought an erotic exploration of the sweet depths of her mouth, teasing the delicate ridges of her tongue with the tip of his own in an oral dance that matched the rhapsody created by his hands as they drifted with sensual sensitivity over her aroused skin.

She lost track of time, of place, as he submitted her to an erotic tasting of such exquisite proportion that her entire body began to ache with the need for fulfilment, and she began to move, silently enticing his possession.

His lips settled in the vulnerable hollow at the base of her throat, then trailed slowly down to the gentle swell of her breast, and she cried out as he took the engorged peak into his mouth and began a tender suckling that slowly intensified until it became a physical torment.

Kristi was unaware of the soft groan emerging from her throat as she reached for him, instinctively begging him in a voice she didn't recognise as her own.

Wild, pagan need consumed her as he began an intimate exploration, his touch attacking the fragile tenure of her control until she began to sob in helpless despair.

Then with one slow movement he entered her, his hard length enclosed by a tight sweetness that took his breath away.

She clung to him, unashamedly caught in the deep, undulating rhythm as she instinctively matched him stroke for stroke, exulting in the sensation that radiated through her body with such exquisite exhilaration.

Pagan, she acknowledged seconds later as he tipped her over the edge, then joined her there in a shuddering climax of his own.

Kristi was supremely conscious of every nerve-end, every cell in her body as she became filled with a languorous warmth, and she cradled his large frame close, loving the feel of his weight, the heat of his skin, slick with the sweat of his passion.

His heart beat strong and fast close to her own, and she sought his mouth, initiating a kiss which soon became *his* as he deepened her soft foray, changing it to something that staked his possession and branded her his own.

Afterwards he rolled onto his back, carrying her with him, and she arched her body, laughing softly as she felt his immediate response.

His hands slid up her ribcage and cradled her breasts, testing their weight as he began to caress each peak with the pad of his thumb, delighting in her reaction as she threw back her head.

Erotic abandon, she admitted a long time later, unsure whether to be pleased or dismayed that she'd become a begging wanton in his arms as he'd led her down a path to sensual conflagration.

'Should we get up, do you think?' Kristi queried as she lay in his embrace.

'I can't think of one good reason why right at this moment,' Shalef drawled, moving his head to brush his lips against her shoulder.

'Lunch?' she offered hopefully.

He bit her gently, then inched his way to the edge of her neck, nuzzling in a manner that sent a renewed surge of sensation arrowing through her body. 'We could have an early dinner.'

'Alternatively, I could go into the kitchen and bring us back a snack.'

'You're hungry for food?' he asked, and she responded teasingly,

'I need to keep up my strength.'

He levered himself easily off the bed and reached for his clothes. 'Stay here,' he commanded gently.

A slow, witching smile curved her lips, and her eyes sparkled with amusement. 'I wasn't planning on going anywhere.'

Shalef returned with a tray of chicken, salad and fresh fruit. After they'd eaten they talked, discussing anything and everything from early childhood memories to world politics, books, movies, art. Then they made leisurely love, and she became an avid pupil beneath his tutorage, taking pleasure from the depth of passion that she was able to arouse.

When the sun began to descend in the sky they rose from the bed, shared the spa-bath, then dressed and went to the dining room for dinner. And later, when the stars shone bright in an inky night sky, they made passionate love until sleep overcame desire.

It became the pattern for the next three days. Days that were filled with lovemaking and laughter, and with the passing of each night Kristi became more aware that to walk away from this man would bring unimaginable heartache.

Seize each moment, a tiny voice bade her. Treasure it and hold it close.

Yet such time-honoured axioms did nothing to help her sense of approaching despair. They couldn't stay here for ever. Sooner or later a phone call or a fax would summon Shalef back to the palace.

It happened on the morning of the fourth day. They arrived back from their early-morning ride to find a servant waiting for them with a cryptic fax which had come through in their absence. Shalef scanned it, then folded the sheet in three and thrust it into the side-pocket of his *thobe*.

'We have to return to Riyadh. Negotiations for your brother's release have been successful.'

Kristi couldn't believe it. 'Shane is to be freed?' Her face mirrored the immense surge of joy that tore through her body. 'How? When? *Where*?'

'Later today. He'll be transported out of the country and receive debriefing before being put on a plane to London.'

'When will I be able to see him?'

'The media circus will begin within hours of his arrival in England, I imagine,' Shalef declared as they crossed the compound. He cast her a dark, probing look. 'It would be advisable for you to be there before he arrives.'

Kristi felt her heart sink. Within a very short time the helicopter would deposit them at the palace. In less than twenty-four hours she would be on a plane to London.

Mission accomplished.

'I agreed to pay any expenses.'

His eyes darkened with anger. 'You insult me.'

'*Why*?' she demanded.

'I requested a favour from a friend,' he said silkily, 'without any pressure that it be granted.' He looked as if he wanted to shake her. 'There was no cost that you have not repaid me.'

Kristi absorbed his words, and felt part of her slowly die. It took tremendous effort to summon a smile, but she managed a passable facsimile. 'Thank you.'

Shalef inclined his head in silent acknowledgement, his eyes hooded, his features assuming a harsh mask.

It was over. The words echoed inside her brain like a death-knell. Without a word she turned and followed him indoors, showered, collected her spare set of clothes, and was ready to board the helicopter when it arrived less than an hour later.

CHAPTER NINE

THE wheels of the large Boeing hit the tarmac, accompanied by the shrill scream of brakes as the passenger jet decelerated down the runway, then cruised into its designated bay at Heathrow airport.

Kristi moved through the terminal, showed her passport, then made her way to the revolving carousel, waited for her luggage to come through, collected it and completed Customs.

Securing a taxi was achieved without delay, and Kristi sank into the rear seat as the driver stowed her bags in the boot. Minutes later the vehicle eased forward into the queue of traffic seeking exit from the busy terminal.

The weather was dull and overcast, cool after the heat of Riyadh, and she fixed her attention beyond the windscreen as the taxi moved smoothly along the bitumen.

A complexity of emotions racked her body, not the least of which was relief that Shane was safe.

Saying goodbye to Shalef as she'd transferred from his Lear jet onto a commercial flight in Bahrain had been the most difficult part of all. Despite her resolve to keep their parting low-key, his brief, hard kiss had stung her lips, and his words of farewell had held the courteous tones of a business associate rather than the emotional intensity of a lover.

What did you expect? she demanded silently. You were attracted to the man, succumbed to his magnetic sex appeal, and shared a few days and nights of passion. Don't fool yourself it was anything other than that.

A week from now you'll be back in Australia, and a romantic interlude in the desert with a Saudi Arabian sheikh of English birth will gradually fade into obscurity.

But she knew that she'd never be able to forget him, and that no man could take his place.

Love, desire, passion. Were the three interdependent, or could they be separated and judged alone? The cold, hard fact was that women were far more prey to emotions than men.

Kristi viewed the streets of London, the traffic, and watched dispassionately as the taxi slid into the wide parking bay adjacent to her centrally placed hotel.

Within a matter of minutes a porter had taken charge of her bag and she was traversing the wide carpeted foyer to Reception.

On being shown to her room she unpacked only what was necessary, discarded her clothes, took a long, hot shower, then opted for a few hours' sleep, for despite it being mid-morning her body-clock was attuned to a different time-zone and she hadn't closed her eyes during the long flight.

When she woke it was early evening, and she donned a robe, made herself a cup of tea, then perused the room-service menu. After dinner she'd ring Sir Alexander Harrington and apprise him of Shane's release.

At nine she switched on the television and alternated channels until way past midnight, slept briefly, then rose and showered ready for an early breakfast.

Loath to venture far from the hotel in case a message came in regarding Shane's expected arrival, she met Georgina in one of the hotel's restaurants for an extended lunch.

'*Tell* me,' Georgina cajoled when they had eaten the entrée, done justice to the main course, and were partway through a delicious concoction of fresh fruit and ice cream.

Kristi lifted her head and met her friend's teasing smile. 'Tell you what?'

'Shane's release is wonderful. It made the initial subterfuge worthwhile.' Georgina's eyes sparkled with intense interest as she leaned forward. 'But give me the details on Shalef bin Youssef Al-Sayed.'

'What details?'

'I refuse to believe you weren't attracted to the man.'

It would have been so easy to confide in a trusted friend, but to do so would only have caused Kristi pain and, perhaps, a feeling of regret. 'He was a very gracious host,' she said carefully.

'Kristi,' Georgina admonished her, 'you're being evasive.'

'OK, what do you want me to say? That he's a wildly sensual man who has women falling at his feet with practically every step he takes?' As you did, a silent voice taunted. She'd been gone two days. Had he contacted any one of his many women friends in Riyadh—*Fayza*?—dined with her, perhaps sated his sexual appetite in her bed? Dear God, even the thought made her feel physically ill.

'Aren't you going to finish dessert?'

Kristi collected herself together. 'No. Shall we order coffee?'

That evening she dined with Sir Alexander and Georgina, and when she returned to the hotel there was a coded message indicating that Shane was due to arrive the following morning.

Sleep was almost impossible and caught in intermittent snatches. With no knowledge of what flight he'd be on, or where it was coming from, she could only wait.

The telephone call came through shortly before midday, and at the sound of her brother's voice all the pent-up emotion culminated in a rush of tears.

'You're in the same hotel?' She couldn't believe it, wouldn't believe it until she saw him. 'What floor, what room number?'

'Order a meal from Room Service, a magnum of champagne, and give me twenty minutes to shower and shave,' Shane instructed, adding gently, 'Then I'll join you.'

He made it in fifteen, and once inside her room he swooped her up in a bear hug and swung her round in a circle before depositing her on her feet. 'Hi there.' His smile was the same, his laughter as bright as ever, but he looked tired and he'd lost weight. He was tall, his hair darker than hers—a deep brown with a hint auburn—and he had strong features and a skin texture that bore exposure to the sun.

'Hi, yourself,' Kristi said softly, leading him to the table set at one end of the room. The food had arrived only minutes before, and she watched as he took a seat, uncorked the champagne, then filled two flutes.

'Here's to being back in one piece.'

'Unharmed?'

'As you see.'

'I think,' Kristi ventured unsteadily, 'you'd better consider assignments in less politically volatile countries. I don't want to go through this again in a hurry.'

His eyes—deep brown flecked with topaz like her own—speared hers. 'Point taken. Off the record, whose influence did you employ to gain my release?'

'Shalef bin Youssef Al-Sayed's.'

An expressive, soft whistle escaped his lips. 'Should I ask how you made contact with him?'

'Initially through Sir Alexander Harrington.'

'And?'

She effected a faint shrug. 'I gave my word.' There was no need to say why, or to whom. Shane possessed the same degree of integrity with *his* sources.

'Do I get to meet Al-Sayed?'

'Possibly. Maybe.' She lifted a hand and smoothed back her hair. 'I'm not sure.'

He noted the nervous gesture, the faint tenseness at the edge of her mouth, and clenched his teeth. If she'd been hurt, by *anyone*, there would be hell to pay.

'So, tell me what happened,' Kristi encouraged, and Shane took up the story from the time of his capture. She recognised the holes he failed to fill, and accepted them.

'This afternoon a statement will be issued to the media,' he concluded with weary resignation. 'I'll be caught up with interviews, television. Then I fly back to Sydney tomorrow afternoon.'

'So soon?'

'The Australian media will want their piece of the action,' he said wryly. 'Then I'm going to lie low for a while.'

'Maybe I can get the same flight,' she said pensively. It seemed an age since she'd left home, and she wanted to resume her life from where she'd left off... how long ago? Five weeks? It felt like half a lifetime.

'No. That wouldn't be advisable. Give it a few days, then follow me.'

She looked at him carefully, seeing the visible signs of strain and tiredness, and expressed her concern. 'You should get some sleep.'

'I will. I'll ring through when I can, but it may not be until tomorrow morning,' he warned as he stood up.

Kristi saw him out, then closed the door behind him.

* * *

Within hours of Shane's departure Kristi secured a flight for Sydney for a few days ahead. Once the booking had been made and she had her ticket, her leaving seemed more of a reality.

Filling those days required little effort as Georgina took charge, first of all dragging her into Harrods, then following it with dinner and a show. The following morning was devoted to attending a beauty parlour for a massage, facial, pedicure, manicure, followed by lunch and a movie.

'Tonight is *mine*,' Kristi declared as they emerged from the cinema in the late afternoon. 'I'm going back to the hotel, ordering room service, followed by an early night.' She gave her friend a stern look. 'And no arguments. I have a long flight ahead of me tomorrow afternoon.'

'So what? You sleep on the plane.' Georgina was carried away with enthusiasm. 'We could go to a nightclub.'

'And get home at three in the morning? No, thanks.'

'It's your last night in town,' Georgina protested. 'You can't spend it alone.'

'Watch me.'

'You leave me no choice but to ring Jeremy and have him take me out.'

'Enjoy,' Kristi bade her, offering a wicked grin, and Georgina laughed.

'I will, believe me.' She leaned forward and pecked Kristi's cheek. 'You only have a block to walk to the hotel. I'll catch a taxi. See you at the airport tomorrow.'

It was almost six when Kristi entered the hotel foyer and took the lift to her floor. There were no messages, and she ordered room service, then stripped off her clothes and pulled on a robe.

Her meal arrived, and she picked at it, then pushed the plate aside. Television failed to hold her interest, and at ten she cleansed her face of make-up, brushed her teeth then slid into bed, only to lie awake staring at the ceiling, fervently wishing that she had agreed to go out with Georgina. At least the bright lights and loud music would have done something to alleviate this dreadful sense of despondency.

She must have fallen asleep, and when she woke the next morning it was late. A shower did much to restore her equanimity, and she ordered breakfast, then made a start with her packing.

A double knock at her door heralded the arrival of Room Service, and she moved across the room to unlock it and allow the waiter access.

But no waiter resembled the tall, dark-haired, immaculately suited man standing in the aperture.

CHAPTER TEN

'SHALEF.' Kristi hadn't realised that it would hurt so much to say his name.

Cool grey eyes raked her slender form, lingered briefly on the soft curve of her mouth, then slid to meet her own. 'Aren't you going to ask me in?'

She dug deep into her resources and managed to display a measure of ease, all too aware of the rapid pulse beat at the base of her throat. 'Would there be any point if I refused?'

'None at all.'

He moved into the room as she stood to one side, and his expression hardened as he saw the open suitcase on the bed.

'You're leaving?'

She looked at him carefully, seeing the inherent strength, the indomitable power that allowed him to shape life in the manner he chose. 'Yes.'

The silence in the room was such that it almost seemed a palpable entity, and her nerves stretched until they felt as taut as a finely strung bow. The sensation angered her unbearably, and she silently damned him for being able to generate such havoc.

He looked at her for what seemed an age, his eyes dark, their inscrutable depths successfully shielding him from any possibility of her gauging his emotions.

When at last he spoke, he appeared to select his words with care. 'We need to talk.'

There wasn't a thing she could say that wouldn't sound inane, so she remained silent, waiting for him to continue.

'I'll be in London for a month, then I fly to Paris,' he revealed. 'I want you with me.'

The breath caught in her throat and threatened to choke her.

'No comment, Kristi?' he queried with a degree of mocking cynicism.

'As what?' Was that her voice? Even to her own ears it sounded impossibly husky. 'Your mistress?'

He didn't answer for several long seconds. 'There are many advantages.'

The tissues around her heart began to tear. Her eyes met his and held them without any effort at all. 'I won't be content with second best, waiting for a stolen night or two whenever you could slip away.' She was breaking in two, and the pain was so intense that she was sure it must be clearly visible to him. Her throat began to ache with the constriction of severe control. 'I would rather not have you at all.'

'Then marry me.'

For a moment she was robbed of the ability to speak. 'Why?' she demanded at last. Her eyes clung to his, searching for some hint of passion, any intensity of emotion by way of reassurance.

'You're a rarity among women of my acquaintance,' Shalef said with quiet emphasis. 'Intelligent, courageous. Equally at ease among the social

glitterati as you are with my Bedu friends in the
desert.'

She closed her eyes in an effort to veil the pain.
'That's hardly a reason for marriage,' she managed
slowly.

'You refuse?'

She looked at him carefully, wanting, needing so
desperately to accept, yet knowing that if she did
she could never be content with good sex and affection as a substitute for love.

It would be so easy to say yes. To accept what
he offered and make do with it. Yet she wanted it
all, and he wasn't ready to give it.

'I'm flying back to Australia on the early-
afternoon flight. Shane is already in Sydney, and
it is more than time we both attempted to attend
to business.'

'You know I will follow you.'

She looked at him with clear eyes, the pain hidden
deep beneath those liquid brown depths. 'Please
don't.' Not unless you love me, she added silently.

'You are prepared to discard what we have
together?'

It will kill me, she thought. 'Without love there
is very little to discard.'

She was mad, *insane* to consider turning him
down. A faint bubble of hysteria rose in her throat
with the knowledge that she had to be the only
woman on any continent in the world who would
consider rejecting Shalef bin Youssef Al-Sayed.

Yet, if she accepted him *now*, it would be akin
to accepting a half-measure. Most—dear heaven,

all women of her acquaintance would be content with less. To have him in their bed, access to his immense wealth and the rewards it would bring would be enough.

'You offer me everything,' Kristi said slowly, and was unable to prevent the faint, husky catch in her voice. Deep inside she felt incredibly sad. She'd hoped for so much, *prayed* that he would say the words she desperately wanted to hear. 'Everything except your love.' Her eyes searched his, hoping to pierce the inscrutable barrier and discover a depth of emotion that was based on more than just desire for her body.

'I want, *need* to be more to you than just a woman gracing your arm, a hostess in your home.' She paused, then added quietly, 'A mistress in your bed.'

There wasn't so much as a flicker in his expression to give any visible indication of his feelings. It angered her unbearably, making her want to rage, *shout*, hit him in order to get some kind of reaction.

'I asked you to be my wife.' The words were softly spoken, yet deadly, and she shivered inwardly as a sliver of ice slid down the length of her spine.

She lifted her head, tilting her head fractionally in silent challenge. 'To bear your sons?' Inside she was slowly dying. 'If you plant only the seeds of daughters in my womb, will you cast me aside for another wife who might sire the son you desire—you *need* to uphold the coveted name of Al-Sayed?'

Icy rage flared briefly in his eyes before it was quickly masked. 'You would lead an envied lifestyle.'

She thought of Nashwa and her daughters, and knew she could never be meekly accepting of such subjugation.

'It isn't enough,' Kristi offered with incredible sadness, aware that life without him would be like dying a very slow and painful death. 'When I marry, I want to believe it will be for ever. That *I* am as important to the man I accept as my husband as he is to me.' Her eyes felt as if they were drowning in unshed tears. 'Above all others. Beyond material possessions.' The ache in her throat was a palpable lump she dared not attempt to swallow. 'I need to know I am everything you need. All you ever want.' She felt boneless, and in danger of falling in an ignominious heap at his feet.

'You ask for guarantees, when with human emotions there can be none? Assurances are only words, given at a time when the head is ruled by the heart.'

'I feel sorry for you, Shalef. True love is a gift. Priceless.'

'I do not require your sympathy,' he declared with an infinite degree of cynicism.

'No,' she agreed bravely. 'You do not even require me.' It almost killed her to voice the words. 'My position in your life, your bed will be easily filled.'

His eyes narrowed fractionally, their depths so darkly unfathomable that it made her feel immeasurably afraid. 'You play for high stakes.'

Her chin lifted, and it took every ounce of strength she possessed to keep her voice level. 'The highest.'

'And if you lose?'

Kristi was aware of her fragile hold on her emotions. Afterwards, she could cry. But not yet. *'Inshallah,'* she said with quiet simplicity.

A tiny flame leapt in his eyes, flaring briefly before being extinguished beneath the measure of his control.

For one infinitesimal second she thought that he might strike her, so intense was his anger, then she silently damned a vivid imagination. He could employ a far more effective method of retribution if he so chose, without resorting to physical violence.

'You try my patience.'

There were words she could have uttered, but they were meaningless phrases, and not worth uttering. 'Please.' She lifted a hand, then let it fall helplessly down to her side. 'I have to finish packing.'

His eyes resembled dark shards of slate as he thrust one hand into his trouser pocket in a tightly controlled gesture.

'You want me to leave?'

'Yes.'

His facial muscles tensed over sculptured bone. 'As you please. But first—'

He reached for her, and she froze, her eyes widening with an apprehension that had little to do with fear as he lowered his head to hers.

The touch of his mouth was soft against her own, and she was unaware of the tiny, inarticulate sound that emerged from her throat as the edge of his tongue made an exploratory sweep over the full curve of her lower lip.

She wanted to cry out, Don't do this to me. A treacherous warmth invaded her veins, firing her body with a passion that she knew she'd never experience with any other man.

It was like drowning, descending with exquisite slowness into a nirvana-like state where reality faded into obscurity. There was only *now*, and the wealth of sensation that he was able to evoke.

Her body shook slightly as she fought against giving a response, and she felt the ache of unshed tears as he alternately teased and cajoled, pressing home with each small advantage gained, until her mouth aligned with his in involuntary capitulation.

A despairing groan rose and died in her throat as he deepened the kiss, possessing, demanding, *invading* in a manner that made her body tremble, and she clutched at his shoulders in a desperate bid to cling onto something tangible as he swept her into an emotional void from which she doubted she could emerge intact.

His passionate intensity was almost a violation, and when he released her she stood perfectly still, afraid that the slightest movement would rend every crack in her crumbling composure.

Part of her wanted to scream, *Go*; get out of my life before I break into a thousand pieces; the other part wanted to beg him to utter the necessary words that would bind her to him for ever.

His eyes were dark and partly hooded, making it impossible to read anything in his expression.

Lifting a hand to her face, he trailed a forefinger lightly over the swollen curves of her mouth, then traced a path along the edge of her jaw and back again.

For what seemed an age he simply looked at her, imprinting on his mind her delicate features, the flawless skin, waxen-pale from the intensity of her emotions, the wide-spaced, fathomless deep brown and topaz eyes, and the bruised softness of her mouth.

Then his hand dropped to his side, and he turned towards the door, walking to it, through it without so much as a backward glance.

The sound of the lock clicking into place proved the catalyst for the release of her tears, and she stood exactly where he'd left her as their flow trickled to each corner of her mouth, then slowly slid to her chin.

Kristi stayed locked into immobility for a very long time, then something stirred within her, providing her with sufficient strength to turn and walk back into the bedroom, where she methodically completed her packing.

She even managed to bathe her face and apply fresh make-up before crossing to the in-house phone and alerting Reception that her bags were ready to be taken down.

'Thank you, Miss Dalton. A car is waiting.'

One last check round the suite, then she caught up her shoulder bag and moved out into the hallway. The lift transported her down to Reception, where she was informed that her account had already been settled.

Her fingers shook as she put away her credit card then handed over the key. Shalef. Like the sleek Bentley parked by the kerb outside the main entrance, with its boot open ready to receive her luggage, it represented a final gesture. A silent, mocking attestation to what she had given up.

Kristi stepped through the revolving door and out into the cool air, and the chauffeur opened the rear passenger door.

She didn't hesitate as she crossed to his side. 'Please thank Sheikh bin Youssef Al-Sayed for his kindness,' she said firmly, 'and tell him that I chose to hire a taxi.'

The chauffeur paled with concern. 'Miss Dalton, I have strict instructions to drive you to the airport and assist you through Customs.'

She offered a faint smile of dismissal. 'That won't be necessary.'

'The Sheikh will be annoyed.'

'With me,' she clarified. One eyebrow rose in wry amusement. 'I don't imagine his instructions included bundling me into the car against my will?'

'No, Miss Dalton.'

'Then you are exonerated from any blame.' Turning away, she spoke to the porter and had him beckon a hovering taxi.

Within minutes it pulled out into the flow of traffic and Kristi leaned back against the seat and stared blindly out of the window. There were people briskly walking on the pavements, coats caught tightly closed against the cold. And it began to rain, settling into a heavy deluge that diminished visibility and set the wipers swishing vigorously back and forth against the windscreen.

In less than twenty-four hours she would touch down to warm summer temperatures, soft balmy breezes, and *home*. The prospect of seeing Shane again, and a few very close friends, should have evoked anticipatory pleasure. Instead, she was filled with a desolation so acute that it became a tangible pain, tearing at her insides and leeching the colour from her face.

CHAPTER ELEVEN

'ANYTHING of interest in next week's bookings?' Kristi queried as she deposited her camera-case on a nearby chair.

'Nothing outstanding,' Shane relayed as he scanned the appointment book spread out on the desk.

It was late, Annie had left for the day, commuters were on their way home, and outside a traffic lull had emptied the streets.

Soon it would be dark, bright neon signs would vie for attention, and the restaurants and theatres would fill with people seeking food, fun and laughter.

Kristi had been back in Sydney for more than a month. Six weeks, three days and counting, she mused idly as she crossed the floor and stood gazing idly out over the city's skyscape.

The inner harbour waters were a brilliant, sparkling blue beneath the sun's rays, their surface dotted with a mix of pleasure craft, two ferries sailing in opposite directions and a huge freighter led by a pilot tug *en route* to a harbour dock.

Two days after her return from London she'd thrown herself into work, taking every assignment that was logged into her appointment book in an effort to keep busy during the daylight hours so that she wouldn't have time to *think*.

She had even let it be known that she was prepared to cover the social circuit, and as a consequence she'd been out most nights at one function or another, photographing some of the city's glitterati. Two weddings, two christenings...the list was far too lengthy, the pace too frenetic for one person alone.

The sun's warmth had coloured her skin a light honey-gold, but her eyes held shadows of sadness, her seldom offered smile lacked any real warmth, and her soft curves had become redefined into almost waif-like slenderness.

She could cope, she assured herself silently. She *had* to cope. The nights were the worst—hours when she lay awake staring into the darkness, *remembering*, caught up with visions so graphic, so explicit that it became an agony of the mind as well as of the flesh.

'I've had an offer which I'm tempted to accept,' Shane offered slowly, hating the shadows beneath her eyes, the carefully contrived smile, and the hint of sadness apparent whenever she thought no one was looking.

'Hopefully not in the wilds of Africa, or Bosnia?' Despite her lightly voiced query, there was an underlying concern. Neither location was an impossibility.

'New Zealand. A geographic spread for the tourism industry. It'll provide a contrast to my last assignment,' he noted with wry humour. 'As a bonus I get to go skiing and trek the Milford Sound.'

She turned back to face him. 'When do you leave?'

'How well you know me,' came the slightly wry observation. 'Tomorrow. Is that a problem?'

'When will you be back?'

'The end of next week, providing the weather holds and there are no delays.' His expression softened. 'Why don't you cancel a few appointments and take some time off? You look ragged.'

'Thanks.' She managed a smile that didn't fool him in the slightest. 'Just what I needed to hear.'

'Hey,' Shane chided her gently. Lifting a hand, he brushed his knuckles along the edge of her jaw. 'I care.'

A smile trembled at the edge of her lips. 'I know.'

'Shalef bin Youssef Al-Sayed may have been instrumental in saving my hide,' he said quietly, 'but if I could get my hands on him now I'd kill him for whatever it is that he's done to you.'

Her eyes were remarkably steady as she met his. 'He wanted marriage,' she said evenly. 'For all the wrong reasons.'

'You love him.'

It was a statement she didn't bother to deny. For as long as she could remember they'd shared an affinity, an extra perception that transcended the norm. It generated an indestructible bond—two minds so attuned to each other's thoughts that there had rarely been the need to explain an action.

'It isn't enough.' Her eyes felt large and ached with suppressed emotion.

'The man is a fool,' Shane said gently.

There had been no phone call, no fax. But then, she hadn't expected any. You lie, a tiny voice taunted. Admit you hoped he would initiate some form of contact. Shalef bin Youssef Al-Sayed was a master player, and she hadn't played the game according to his plan. There were a hundred other women who could fill his bed. Ten times that many who would leap at the chance.

Kristi switched on the answering machine and caught up her camera-bag. 'Let's lock up and get out of here.'

'Dinner. Somewhere that serves good food,' Shane suggested as he followed her to the door.

'I'd rather go home.'

He tended the lock, checked that it was firmly in place, then moved ahead of her down the single flight of stairs. 'A restaurant. I'm buying. And don't argue,' he added softly as they reached the pavement.

French cuisine at its best, Kristi mused almost two hours later. Despite her professed lack of appetite, she'd managed to do justice to chicken consommé followed by a delectable portion of steamed fish with a delicate lemon sauce, accompanied by an assortment of vegetables. To finish, she'd selected a compote of fresh fruit doused in brandy, then flambéed and served with cream.

'Coffee?'

'Please,' she said gratefully. 'Black, very strong.' A few months ago she would have requested a decaffeinated variety and added milk. How some things change, she mused idly as she pushed down the plunger of the cafetière and poured the dark, aromatic brew into two cups. Adding a liberal amount of sugar, she sank back in her chair, then lifted the cup to her lips and took an appreciative mouthful.

The glass of Cabernet Shiraz she'd sipped throughout the meal had had a mellowing effect. 'Thanks.'

'For dinner?'

Kristi smiled. 'For insisting on bringing me here.'

'My pleasure.'

It was late, she was tired, and she knew that she really should go home, but she was loath to return to her empty apartment. So she finished her coffee and poured another for herself and for Shane.

'Want to talk about it?' he queried lightly, and she shook her head.

'Then let's do the business thing. What do you think about allowing Annie to buy a small share of the studio?'

'You're serious?'

'You have reservations?'

'It's been Dalton Photographics for years,' she protested. 'Why change?'

'It will still be Dalton Photographics.'

Comprehension dawned as she remembered the faintly wistful expression on a certain young woman's face whenever Shane was in town. *'Annie?'*

'Is it so obvious?'

'Not to anyone else.' A slow, sweet smile lit her features. 'I can't think of anyone I'd rather have as a sister-in-law.'

'I proposed last night. When I get back from New Zealand we'll make it official. More coffee?'

She shook her head, and he beckoned for the account, then checked off each item, signed, and handed over a tip as he got to his feet.

He took her key as they reached their parked vehicles, unlocked her door, then saw her safely seated behind the wheel with her belt in place.

'Drive carefully.'

She cast him a teasing glance. 'Always,' she assured him. 'Don't fall off the side of a mountain.'

'No chance.' He reached out a hand and brushed his fingers against her cheek. 'I'll phone.'

'Make sure of it.' She turned the key in the ignition and fired the engine, then put the car into gear. *'Ciao.'*

It took fifteen minutes to reach her apartment, another fifteen for her to shower and slip into bed.

Perhaps it was the wine or the numerous sleepless nights but the next thing she heard was the sound of her alarm the following morning.

Annie was on the phone when Kristi walked into the studio shortly after eight, and in comical sign language she indicated that there was hot coffee in the percolator and could Kristi pour one for her too.

Annie should have opted for a career on the stage, Kristi mused as she extracted two mugs, added sugar, filled each with the hot, deliciously aromatic brew and deposited a mug on Annie's desk. The girl was a natural-born satirist who could mimic anyone you cared to name.

'Miss Dalton,' Annie reiterated in a low, devilishly husky voice as soon as she replaced the receiver, her eyes sparkling with impish humour, 'is summoned to undertake a photographic session at one of *the* most fabulous homes Point Piper has to offer. An interior decorator is being flown in from London *after* she's sighted photographs of each room, the existing landscaping, and the exterior shot from every imaginable angle.'

'When?'

'One gets the feeling it should have been yesterday. I said that you couldn't possibly fit him in until this afternoon.'

Kristi took an appreciative sip of coffee. 'And?'

'He negotiated for this morning.'

'What did you say?'

'I almost considered rescheduling. But he sounded...' She paused, then continued with dramatic intonation, 'frightfully autocratic. I decided he deserved to be taught a little humility.'

'You're incorrigible.'

'I know. I need taking in hand,' she declared with humour, and Kristi gave a subdued laugh.

'Shane assures me he is in line to do just that.' Her features softened with genuine affection. 'I'm delighted for both of you.'

Annie's eyes acquired an extra sparkle. 'Thanks. It'll be a small wedding, just immediate family. Shane wants it to happen three days after he returns from New Zealand.' Her smile widened into a mischievous grin. 'I'm plumping for the end of the month.'

'It will be interesting to see who wins.'

'I'll have fun enjoying Shane's method of persuasion.'

Kristi experienced a shaft of pain at Annie's obvious happiness, and endeavoured to bury it deep beneath the surface. 'I don't imagine he'll find cause for complaint.'

The strident sound of the phone interrupted their conversation and Annie snatched up the receiver, spoke into it at length, scanned the appointment book, made a booking, then concluded the call.

'Now, where were we?'

'Our so-named autocratic client,' Kristi reminded her. 'What if he wants shots of the pool reflecting the early-morning sun?'

'You develop this afternoon's film then shoot tomorrow,' Annie rationalised, raising her hands in an expressive gesture. 'As long as the courier picks up before five they'll be on a flight out of here tomorrow night.'

'You were able to convince him of that?'

'He didn't threaten to use one of the competition.'

'What time am I supposed to be there?'

'One-thirty. He didn't even query the fee.'

Kristi shot her a sharp look. 'Tell me you didn't load it.'

'*Moi*?' Annie queried with mock humour. 'I simply informed him there was an extra charge for a rush job.'

'What would I do without you?'

'Survive,' the vivacious brunette responded with a sunny smile.

Kristi finished the last of her coffee, then rinsed and put away the mug before checking the appointment book. 'Bickersby, studio, eight-thirty, followed by a ten-thirty session at a client's home in Clontarf. Children's photographs.' She would have enough time to finish, return to the studio, grab some lunch, then be at Point Piper by one-thirty.

Annie was right—the house was fabulous, Kristi decided a few hours later as she parked her car in a street lined with prestigious homes. Some had been there a long time, while there were a few huge modern structures which had obviously replaced the original houses, comprising three and sometimes four levels against the sloping cliff-face. The view out over the harbour was spectacular, and the price-tag for each home would run into several millions of dollars.

She ran a quick check of the house number, then alighted from the car, collected her gear, and approached the security intercom attached to an ornate steel gate.

At the front door a housekeeper greeted her and led the way through a spacious foyer to an informal lounge.

The interior was a little too ascetic for Kristi's taste. There should have been artwork on the walls, bowls filled with freshly cut flowers, and the primrose-painted walls needed be repainted in cool off-white or pale calico to emphasise the light, airy design.

'My employer requested that I convey his apologies. He's been delayed by a business call which may take up to ten minutes. Would you like a cool drink or a cup of coffee or tea while you wait?'

'Tea would be lovely, thanks.' Lunch had been an apple eaten *en route* from her previous booking. Photographing children was a hazardous occupation, for they tended to be unpredictable when faced with a stranger wielding a camera. This morning's session had run badly over time, with a harried young mother professing that it would be *years* before she could contemplate assembling her normally angelic little darlings for another professional sitting. Despite Kristi's efforts to capture their amusement with a hand puppet, the children, aged eighteen months, three and four years, had collectively gone from shy to awkward to uncooperative, resorted to tears, then finally succumbed to blatant bribery.

There was a sense of relief, Kristi mused wryly, in that this afternoon's booking involved an inanimate house. Crossing to the wide glass window, she turned back and checked the light, mentally choosing the best angles.

The housekeeper appeared with a tray which she set down on a low table. 'I'll leave you to pour.' She indicated a plate of delicately prepared sandwiches. 'Just in case you're hungry.'

Kristi gave an appreciative smile. 'Thanks. I missed lunch.'

The tea was Earl Grey, the sandwiches smoked salmon and cream cheese. Divine, she described them silently as she bit into another and replaced her cup on the tray.

She would have liked to wander through the house while she waited, observing and conducting a professional assessment. It would save time.

With ideal contemplation she wondered at the identity of the new owner. The house was only a few years old, and its design held the stamp of one of Sydney's finest architects whose brilliance commanded an exorbitant fee. Despite the colours not being her personal preference, the workmanship was superb. The fact that he was employing an international interior decorator indicated that no expense would be spared in establishing the owner's individual taste.

'Miss Dalton?'

Kristi turned at the sound of the housekeeper's voice.

'I'll take you down to the office now.'

They descended to the next level via a wide, curved staircase which led to a spacious marble-tiled area complete with an ornate fountain centrally positioned beneath a crystal chandelier. The housekeeper indicated a hallway to her left.

'The office is situated at the end, the last door on the right.'

There was no logical reason for the faint unfurling of nerves inside Kristi's stomach or the prickle of apprehension that settled between her shoulderblades as she drew closer.

Crazy, she dismissed as the housekeeper paused beside the closed door and knocked before standing to one side.

'Please go in, Miss Dalton.'

A faint shiver shook her slim frame, yet her hand was steady as she turned the handle and pushed open the door.

It was a large room, she saw at once, complete with an assortment of high-tech electronic business equipment. Bookcases lined one wall, and the desk was an expensive antique.

Behind it the high-backed swivel-chair was empty, and her eyes slid to a tall figure silhouetted against the floor-to-ceiling plate-glass window.

The man's height and breadth looked achingly familiar, and the breath caught in her throat as she willed him to turn and face her.

Almost as if he sensed her apprehension, he shifted, his movements deliberately slow as he swung away from the window.

Shalef.

There was something primitive in his expression, and every instinct she possessed warned of the need for caution. It vied with a slow-burning anger that made her want to demand a reason for his presence in Sydney—more particularly, *why* he had summoned her to this house.

Innate dignity put a temporary rein on her temper as she studied his features, noting the fine lines fanning out from the corners of his eyes, the chiselled perfection of his mouth, the slashes down each cheek that seemed more deeply etched than she remembered.

Superbly tailored black trousers accentuated the muscular length of his legs, while the white silk shirt lent emphasis to his height and breadth of shoulder. He had loosened the top three buttons of his neck and folded back both cuffs, lending a casual, relaxed look that was belied by the most electric energy projected with effortless ease.

It was an energy that both thrilled and frightened, for she'd witnessed it unfurled and at its most dangerous.

Now she was unsure of its measure, and of his precise reason for requesting her presence.

It took considerable effort to inject her voice with polite civility. 'There are any number of competent photographers listed in the telephone directory capable of providing the services you require.' She drew in a deep breath, then released it slowly. 'It would better if you contacted one of them.'

One dark eyebrow lifted slightly and his smile was faintly cynical. 'Better for whom?'

If he was going to play games, she'd turn around and walk out *now*. 'Shalef—'

'I was assured by your secretary that the photographs would be ready early this evening,' he declared with dangerous silkiness. 'Are you now implying that you intend to renege on a verbal business agreement?'

Professionalism and sheer inner strength brought a lift to her chin and lent her eyes an angry sparkle. She'd complete the session and provide him with his wretched photographs, if only to prove that he no longer possessed the power to affect her. 'Perhaps you could tell me precisely what you want, then I can get started.'

He didn't move, but she sensed his body muscles tense with restrained anger.

'I return to London tomorrow. I'd prefer to take the prints with me.'

Her eyes flashed with brilliant fire. 'Why a London interior decorator? What's wrong with employing an Australian firm?'

'I have utilised this firm's services for a number of years.' He paused, then continued quietly, 'I trust their judgement and have no qualms about leaving them to complete everything to my satisfaction in my absence.'

Pain knotted in the region of her stomach, and she had to consciously stop herself from gasping out loud. After tonight she'd never see him again.

'Very well.'

He shifted away from the desk and walked to the door. 'We'll begin outside while the light is still good.'

Instead of choosing the staircase, he led the way to a cleverly concealed lift, and in the cubicle's close confines she could feel the fast hammering of her heart. A tell-tale pulse beat in unison at the base of her throat, and she had to fight the temptation to cover it with a protective hand.

There were five buttons on the indicator panel, and she almost cried out in relief when the lift slid to a smooth halt on the lowest level.

Focus, concentrate, she commanded herself silently as she walked at his side through a large, informal area to wide, sliding glass doors opening out onto a terracotta-tiled patio and a free-form swimming pool.

For the next ten minutes Kristi reeled off numerous shots of the pool, external frontage from several angles and the view out over the harbour, before moving inside.

Shalef was never far from her side, suggesting, directing, asking her opinion on occasion as she steadily filled one roll of film, then paused to remove it and insert another.

It was a game, she decided in desperation. Deliberately orchestrated by a man who had no concern for the emotional storm that tore at her insides and ripped her nerves to shreds.

Twice his arm brushed against one of hers, and the faint muskiness of his cologne combined with his masculine scent almost succeeded in driving her insane.

It seemed for ever before the interior shooting was completed, and she welcomed the fresh, cooling breeze as she moved outdoors and shot the house from the street, the gardens, the driveway.

'That's it,' Kristi announced finally, aware that she had far more than she could possibly need. With care she capped the lens and removed the strap from her neck. Her shoulders felt slightly stiff and she had the beginnings of a headache. Tension, from being in Shalef bin Youssef Al-Sayed's company for the past few hours—three, she noted with surprise as she spared her watch a quick glance.

'I'll collect my bag from the foyer then get back to the studio.' The sooner she made a start on the developing process, the sooner she'd be finished.

Several minutes later, bag in hand, she moved towards the front door. The knot of tension inside her stomach tightened into a painful ball, and her smile was a mere facsimile of one as she turned towards him. 'I can't give you a definite time. Somewhere between seven and eight o'clock?'

He inclined his head and accompanied her to her car, waiting as she unlocked it; then, when she was seated, he shut the door.

The engine fired immediately and she paused only long enough to secure her seat belt before sending the BMW down the road.

It wasn't until she had gained the main New South Head road that she was able to relax, and even then it was strictly temporary.

'Well? What is he like?' Annie demanded the instant Kristi entered the studio. 'Make my day and tell me he's tall, dark and gorgeous.'

'Any messages?' Kristi crossed to the desk and checked the message pad. 'I'll be in the lab for the next hour. Maybe longer.'

Annie wrinkled her nose in silent admonition, and her eyes sharpened fractionally. 'You look tired. Why don't you go home and come in early in the morning?'

'Because, Annie, darling,' she revealed, 'the client requires the prints tonight.'

'Tell him you can't do it.'

'Too late. I already told him I can.'

'Then I'll make some fresh coffee.'

Kristi gave a smile in thanks. 'You're an angel.'

It was after seven when she examined the last print. With professional dedication she collated them according to floor level, noting each room and its aspect, before pushing them into a large envelope.

Moving her shoulders, she eased the crick in her neck, then massaged each temple in an effort to diminish the dull, aching sensation which had settled there more than an hour ago.

She felt tired, hungry, and would have given almost anything to go home, sink into a spa-bath and have the tiny, pulsing jets work their magic on her tense muscles.

Fifteen minutes later she wound down the window of her car and pressed the security intercom outside the set of high iron gates guarding the entrance to Shalef's harbourfront home. Within seconds they slid open and she eased the car towards the front of the house, parking it right outside the main door... for an easy getaway, she told herself as she retrieved the thick envelope from the passenger seat.

The housekeeper answered the door and Kristi wondered why she should be surprised. Shalef lived in a world where one employed staff to maintain residences. However, this was Sydney, not London or Riyadh.

'Would you please give this to Sheikh bin Al-Sayed?' Kristi requested, holding out the package. 'I've enclosed the account.'

'Sheikh bin Al-Sayed wishes to pay you now. If you'd care to wait in the lounge?'

No, I wouldn't care to wait, Kristi felt like screaming, and I don't want to see Shalef bin Youssef Al-Sayed.

'Thank you, Emily. I'll take care of Miss Dalton.'

She should have known that he wouldn't allow her to get away so easily, she decided in despair. 'I've delivered the prints as you requested,' she ventured quietly.

'Emily has prepared dinner,' Shalef declared smoothly. 'We'll eat, then I'll go through the prints.'

'*No.*' The single negation took the place of a silent, primal scream that sprang from the depths of her soul. 'I can't. I'm expecting a phone call.' She was babbling—short, stark sentences that sounded desperate even to her own ears.

His eyes hardened measurably. 'I imagine whoever it is will leave a message on your answering machine.'

'Damn you, Shalef,' she flung at him, shaky with anger as he took hold of her arm and led her through to an informal dining room where the table was set for two.

Covered dishes had been placed in the centre, and her stomach clenched in hungry anticipation at the delicious aroma permeating the room.

'Sit down.'

It was easier to capitulate, and she made no protest as he uncorked a bottle of Cabernet Shiraz and poured a generous measure into her glass.

'Emily is an exceptional cook,' Shalef informed her as he uncovered a dish and served her a generous portion, adding rice from the second dish. He served himself, then took the seat opposite. 'Eat, Kristi,' he commanded silkily. He filled his own glass, then raised it in a silent toast.

Kristi picked up her fork and speared a delectable piece of chicken. Sautéed in wine and mushrooms, it tasted out of this world.

She thought of a dozen things to say, and discarded every one of them. The wine was superb, and gradually it began to dissipate the knot of tension inside her stomach.

'Why did you buy this house?' Surely the house was a safe subject?

His eyes lingered on her mouth, then slowly traversed the slope of her nose before locking with her own. 'I wanted an Australian base.'

'Extending your global interests?'

'You could say that.'

She was breaking up inside, fragmenting into a hundred pieces. If she didn't gather her shattered nerves together, she'd never be able to get up and walk out of here with any semblance of dignity.

She put down her fork, then carefully replaced her glass. Not carefully enough, for the rim caught the side of her plate and slipped from her fingers. With horrified fascination she watched the wine spill into an ever widening dark pool on the white damask. 'I'm so sorry.' The apology fell from her lips as a whisper. Moisture welled from behind her eyes, distorting her vision as she plucked up her napkin and dabbed it over the spillage. 'The table-cloth should be rinsed or it will stain,' she said shakily.

'Leave it,' he commanded. 'It isn't important.'

'I'll replace it.'

'Don't be ridiculous.'

She closed her eyes, then slowly opened them again. Hell couldn't be any worse than this. 'If you'll excuse me, I'd prefer to leave.' She rose to her feet and sidestepped the chair. 'Thank you for dinner.' It was amazing. Even at a time like this she could still remember good manners.

She turned blindly away from the table, only to be brought to a halt mid-stride by a hand closing over her arm.

His eyes were dark, their expression so deeply inscrutable that it was impossible to discern his mood.

For what seemed an age he just looked at her, his silence unnerving in the stillness of the room.

She was damned if she'd cry. Tears were for the weak and she had to be strong. Her eyes ached as she strove to keep the moisture at bay, and she almost succeeded. Almost—the exception being a solitary tear which overflowed and spilled slowly down one cheek. It came to rest at the corner of her mouth, and after a few long seconds she edged the tip of her tongue out to dispense with it.

A husky, self-deprecating oath fell from his lips, and she stood in mesmerised silence as he caught hold of her hand and carried it to his mouth.

'Dear God,' Shalef groaned. *'Don't.'* His hand moved to capture her shoulders, then slid upwards to stroke her hair. His eyes were dark—so dark that they mirrored her own emotional pain as he held her head.

'For years I have enjoyed feminine company and never had to work at a relationship. *You,*' he enlightened her with gentle emphasis, 'mentally stripped me of all my material possessions and judged me for the man that I am without them. For the first time I had nothing to rely on except myself. It wasn't an enviable situation,' he said with a touch of self-mockery.

Kristi stood perfectly still, almost afraid to move.

'You didn't conform and I was intrigued. I thought I knew every facet of a woman, but you proved me wrong.' He paused, tilting her face slightly so that she had to look at him. 'You opposed me at every turn, and argued without hesitation. Yet you were angelic with Nashwa, sympathetic with Aisha and Hanan. I knew without doubt that I wanted you as my wife.' His expression became faintly wry. 'I imagined all I had to do was ask and you'd agree.'

He smiled, and the first flutter of hope began to stir inside her stomach.

'Instead you refused and walked out on me. My initial instinct was to follow you. Yet if I had then, even if I'd said the words you so wanted to hear, you would have been disinclined to believe them. So I decided to give you time. Not too much, but enough. Enough for me to set up this house and invent a reason to get you here.'

Her lips parted to protest, and he stilled her flow of words very effectively by taking possession of her mouth.

When he finally lifted his head, her own was reeling with the degree of passion he'd managed to evoke.

'This afternoon I wanted to declare my love the instant you walked in the door, but I had to allow for your outrage,' he qualified with genuine regret, 'and crack the protective barrier you'd erected around your heart.' His lips settled against her temple, then trailed a gentle path down to the edge of her mouth.

She felt shaky, and almost afraid to believe his words.

'I have something for you,' Shalef said gently. He withdrew a ring from his trouser pocket and placed it in the palm of her hand. 'It belonged to my mother, gifted to her by my father.'

Kristi looked at the wide gold ring embedded with diamonds.

'She never wore it, preferring a plain gold band, but she accepted it for what it represented...a symbol of my father's love.'

She raised her eyes to meet his, saw the depth of passion evident, and was unable to tear her gaze away.

'It was held in safe-keeping and handed to me on my twenty-fifth birthday, with the relayed request that I gift it to the woman I chose to be my wife.'

'It's beautiful,' Kristi said simply.

He brushed his fingers down her cheek, and warmth radiated through her body, bringing with it the need for the sweet sorcery of his touch.

'Marriage was something I viewed as a convenient necessity with a woman of whom I could become fond...someone who could be my social hostess, the mother of my children, and pleasure me in bed.' He smiled—a slightly wry gesture that was belied by the warm humour evident in the depths of his eyes. 'Then I met you. And every woman of my acquaintance paled in comparison.' He traced the curves of her mouth with a forefinger, and followed its path with his tongue before seeking the soft inner tissues, to create an emotional demand which she didn't hesitate to answer.

When at last he lifted his head she could only look at him in bemusement as she saw the raw need, the hunger and the passion in his eyes.

'I love you. *Love,*' Shalef declared as he slid trembling hands to frame her face.

His eyes were dark, almost black, and Kristi sensed the faint uncertainty in his touch—a vulnerability she'd thought she would never see. It moved her more than she could bear.

'I know the only worthy gift I can bestow on you is my heart,' he said deeply. 'It's yours. For as long as it beats within me.'

Joy unfurled from deep within her and soared to an unbelievable height. Without hesitation she lifted her hands and wound them round his neck.

'I'll take great care of it,' she promised softly.

His features assumed a gentleness that almost made her want to cry. 'And you'll marry me?'

Kristi smiled—a wonderfully warm smile that was meant to banish any doubts. The desire to tease him a little was irresistible. 'Are you asking?'

His faint laugh was low and husky as he gathered her close in against him. 'You want me to go down on bended knee?'

'I may never see you so humbled again,' she ventured solemnly, and he slowly shook his head.

'You're wrong. Each day I'll give thanks that I have the good fortune to share your life.'

She felt the prick of tears, and was unable to still the twin rivulets that ran slowly down each cheek.

'You haven't answered.'

Her mouth trembled. 'Yes.'

His mouth closed over hers, possessing it with such incredible passion that she felt dizzy when he finally lifted his head.

'Will you mind if the civil ceremony in London is followed by another in Riyadh?'

It was somehow fitting, and something that would have pleased his father. She thought of sharing the arrangements with Nashwa, Aisha and Hanan, and knew the enjoyment it would give them.

'Not at all.'

'We'll spend the first week of our honeymoon in Taif, then cruise the Greek islands for a month.'

'June is a nice month for brides,' Kristi offered wistfully.

'Next week,' Shalef commanded. 'You fly out to London with me tomorrow. Don't object,' he ordered as she opened her mouth.

'I could follow in a few days. No?' Her eyes sparkled mischievously. 'The day after?'

'Tomorrow,' he reaffirmed, giving her a gentle shake.

'In that case I'd better go home and pack.'

'All you need is your passport and a change of clothes, which we'll collect from your apartment *en route* to the airport in the morning.' His mouth fastened over hers in a kiss that left her weak-kneed and malleable. 'I have plans for what remains of the night.' He revealed precisely what those plans were, none of which involved any sleep. 'You can rest on the plane,' he added gently as he placed an arm beneath her knees and swung her into his arms.

In the bedroom he lowered her to her feet, and she reached for the buttons on his shirt, slipping them free before tackling the belt at his waist.

Kristi uttered a small gasp as his fingers brushed against her breast, then she groaned out loud as he began teasing each burgeoning peak, intensifying an awareness that radiated from the centre of her being until it encompassed every vein, every sensitised nerve-ending.

She was *his*, wholly, completely, to do precisely whatever he wanted with, and she helped him shed what remained of her clothes while he gave assistance in discarding his own before drawing her down onto the bed.

'My darling,' Shalef whispered with due reverence as he studied the silky sheen of her smooth-textured skin, and his gaze lingered on the soft curves of her breasts, the delicately shaped waist, before settling on the deep auburn curls protecting her womanhood.

He lifted a hand and brushed his fingers back and forth over the soft concavity of her stomach before trailing to trace the bones at one hip.

Her whole body ached with the promise of passion too long denied, and she reached for him.

'I want you *now*,' she whispered fiercely. 'All of you, inside me, without any preliminaries.' She cried out as his fingers slipped beneath the soft curls to initiate a sweet sorcery that quickly tipped her over the edge into a secret place where passion flared into an all-consuming fire, sweeping aside inhibition as it imbued her with an abandon that completely took his breath away as he carefully prepared her to accept his swollen length.

Silken tissues stretched to accommodate him, warm and wonderfully sleek as she met that initial thrust, encouraging his total possession by rising up against him in a rhythm that increased in pace until there was no master, no mistress, only two people in perfect accord, intent on gifting the other with the ultimate pleasure.

Afterwards she rested her cheek against the curve of his shoulder, too satiated to move so much as a muscle as he lightly trailed his fingers up and down the length of her spine.

This time their lovemaking was slow and erotic, ascending to new heights of intoxicating sensuality, and it was almost dawn before they drifted into a deep sleep from which they woke in time to shower, dress and depart for the airport via her apartment.

Once aboard the plane, Kristi slept most of the way to Hawaii, waking to meet the indulgent eyes of the man who would soon be her husband.

'Hello,' she greeted him softly, giving him a smile so warm and so incredibly sweet that it almost robbed him of breath.

Careless of the other passengers travelling in the first-class section of the aircraft, he leaned over and bestowed a lingering kiss on her lips.

'I've booked us into a hotel for a fourteen-hour stopover.'

Her eyes filled with wicked humour. 'Only fourteen hours?'

His mouth softened into a sensual curve. 'You require more than fourteen?'

She reached out a hand and traced the strong sweep of his jawline before covering his cheek with her palm. 'I love you.'

'Now you tell me,' Shalef groaned softly. '*Here*, where I can do very little about it.'

She cast him an angelic smile that was totally at variance with the witching sparkle lighting her eyes. 'Patience, they tell me, is good for the soul.'

His answering gaze was filled with musing self-mockery. 'Patience,' he stressed lightly, 'will doubtless stretch the limit of my control.'

Kristi laughed softly. 'I promise I'll allow you to make up for it.'

One eyebrow rose in a gesture of wry humour. 'That's supposed to get me through dinner, landing, Customs and a three-quarter-hour drive to the hotel?'

Her eyes teased him unmercifully. 'But think of the reward ... for each of us.'

His expression darkened with the promise of renewed passion. 'Indeed,' he agreed gently. 'A lifetime.'

As Seen on TV!

Free Gift Offer

With a Free Gift proof-of-purchase
from any Harlequin® book, you can receive
a beautiful cubic zirconia pendant.

This stunning marquise-shaped stone is a genuine cubic
zirconia—accented by an 18" gold tone necklace.
(Approximate retail value $19.95)

Send for yours today...
compliments of HARLEQUIN®

To receive your free gift, a cubic zirconia pendant, send us one original proof-of-purchase, photocopies not accepted, from the back of any Harlequin Romance®, Harlequin Presents®, Harlequin Temptation®, Harlequin Superromance®, Harlequin Intrigue®, Harlequin American Romance®, or Harlequin Historicals® title available in February, March or April at your favorite retail outlet, together with the Free Gift Certificate, plus a check or money order for $1.65 U.S./$2.15 CAN. (do not send cash) to cover postage and handling, payable to Harlequin Free Gift Offer. We will send you the specified gift. Allow 6 to 8 weeks for delivery. Offer good until April 30, 1997, or while quantities last. Offer valid in the U.S. and Canada only.

Free Gift Certificate

Name: _____

Address: _____

City: _____ State/Province: _____ Zip/Postal Code: _____

Mail this certificate, one proof-of-purchase and a check or money order for postage and handling to: HARLEQUIN FREE GIFT OFFER 1997. In the U.S.: 3010 Walden Avenue, P.O. Box 9071, Buffalo NY 14269-9057. In Canada: P.O. Box 604, Fort Erie, Ontario L2Z 5X3.

FREE GIFT OFFER   084-KEZ

ONE PROOF-OF-PURCHASE

To collect your fabulous FREE GIFT, a cubic zirconia pendant, you must include this original proof-of-purchase for each gift with the properly completed Free Gift Certificate.

084-KEZ

Take 4 bestselling love stories FREE

Plus get a FREE surprise gift!

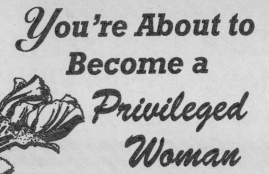

You're About to Become a *Privileged Woman*

Reap the rewards of fabulous free gifts and benefits with proofs-of-purchase from Harlequin and Silhouette books

Pages & Privileges™

It's our way of thanking you for buying our books at your favorite retail stores.

PROOF OF PURCHASE

HP-PP23

Offer expires March 31, 1997

Pages & Privileges ™

Harlequin and Silhouette— the most privileged readers in the world!

For more information about Harlequin and Silhouette's PAGES & PRIVILEGES program call the Pages & Privileges Benefits Desk: 1-503-794-2499

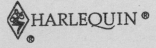

HARLEQUIN ®

HP-PP23